ONE FOR SORROW

D.G. TORRENS

Copyright © 2023 D.G. Torrens

ISBN: 9798393033989

ONE FOR SORROW

Cover design: Cover Collection
Formatting: Damos Jackson
Editor: Scott Bury

To all who suffer at the hands of another:

"Not all scars fade. Some are supposed to stay to remind us that the real beauty lies in surviving them"–

To Jackie
(The Old Joint Stock Birmingham)

Thank you for your kindness and positivity. The best waitress in the city.

Pain does not discriminate.
We are all equal during its devastation.

D.G. Torrens—

CHAPTER ONE

(Present day)

*A*very collapsed at the top of the staircase, furled into a foetal position. Her cheeks drenched in tears and fighting the urge to close her eyes, Avery dug into her jeans pocket for her mobile phone. Barely able to see through her swelling eyes while navigating the keypad. After several attempts, she tapped 999, wincing through each breath drawn. The pain in her ribs stabbed through her every move. Avery placed her hand over her rib cage while struggling to stay awake.

"Emergency. Which service do you require, fire, police, or ambulance?"

"Ambulance. Police," Avery gasped.

"And your name and number?" requested the operator.

Avery faintly revealed her details to the operator.

"I am transferring your call to the force control room. Stay on the line, Avery."

Avery was losing the battle to remain conscious. She laid her head down on the floor.

"Hello Avery, my name is Sofie. Can you state your location for me?"

Silence ensued.

"Avery...are you there?"

Avery's eyes flickered open. The distant sound of a woman's voice echoed through her phone. "I'm here," she whispered.

"Good. You are doing great, Avery. Stay with me. Where are you located?"

"111 Church Street, Finswick. I'm hurt. He's dead..." Avery trailed off. The overwhelming desire to sleep arrested her and unconsciousness prevailed.

"Avery are you still with me?" pressed the operator.

No response.

"If you can hear me, Avery, we have pinpointed your location. Someone is on their way to you."

* * *

Avery's eyes flashed open. The swelling weighed heavily on her eyelids. Her face twisted with each breath drawn. She cradled her rib cage to ease the pain. The crackling of her ribs shook her.

"You're awake! Good. How are you feeling?" asked a nurse, standing at the foot of her bed with a clipboard in hand.

Avery didn't respond. Disorientated, her eyes frantically scoped the room until her eyes rested on the nurse's face. His warm smile focused on Avery.

The nurse noted her concern and attempted to ease her mind. "It's okay. You are in hospital."

The nurse continued. "My name is Aiden. Take it easy and don't move too much."

Avery searched Aiden's face and her eyes rested on his name tag, confirming what he just said.

Aiden offered a warm smile. "You are safe now, Avery."

Aiden hung the clipboard on the foot of the bed, reached for a glass of water off the table, and held the straw to her lips.

"The consultant will be along shortly to speak with you."

Avery's eyes trailed over the young nurse. His fair hair glistened in the sunlight peeking through the blinds. His face, kind and genuine.

"I will be back later to check on you. If you need anything, press the button above your head. It will alert the nurse's station," he advised before exiting the room.

"Wait," she whispered, wincing from the pain in her jaw.

Aiden turned around and walked over to Avery's bed. "You need to be careful. Your jaw has received a hairline fracture. Try not to speak too much. Can I get you something?"

"Was anyone else brought into the hospital with me?"

Aiden offered a warm smile. "Not that I'm aware. I wasn't on duty when you arrived. I can find out for you."

"I'd appreciate that. Thank you, Aiden."

Avery brought her hand to her mouth and cradled it. "Try not to use your mouth too much, okay?" Aiden reiterated.

Avery nodded. Aiden turned and left the room.

A flashback of that night wrought fear in Avery. She panicked, thinking about the possibility that Ethan could still be alive. *No, no, no, it's not possible. He can't be!*

An hour later, Avery's consultant entered her room.

"Hello, my name is Dr Chaudhary. How are you doing today?"

Avery shuffled delicately on her bed. "Okay," she lied, lowering her eyes.

"That's good to hear. It was quite a beating. You have a fractured rib and a minor hairline fracture in your lower jaw. You will need to limit your facial movement and what foods you take for a while to give it time to heal. I will prescribe medication so you can manage your pain." Dr Chaudhary inched forward in his chair.

"I do have some positive news. Your baby is doing fine and did not suffer physically because of the attack on you. Your baby's vitals are stable. We will closely monitor you, to ensure it stays that way." Dr Chaudhary paused, allowing Avery time to process his news.

Her eyes glistened. A single tear trailed down her cheek.

3

"Pregnant? Are you sure?"

"I'm sure."

Avery shook her head. Tears flowed down her cheeks. She raised a hand and swiped them away. "How long?" she managed.

"Seven weeks."

Avery felt numb. It was too much for her mind to process. She stuttered, trying to get her words out. Her body shivered and her hands shook. She attempted to reach for a tissue off the side table.

"Here, let me." Dr Chaudhary reached for a tissue and handed it to Avery.

"Thank you," she struggled through her tears.

"It's okay, Avery. You don't need to think about that right now. The most important thing is your recovery. Your scan results are back and revealed slight head trauma. However, it's not serious or life-threatening. You will have quite the headache for a while though, but we can manage that with pain relief, too. Your rib suffered from a hairline fracture, much like your jaw. It is small and, again, will be painful for a few weeks. You will need to keep the support bandages on. This will ease your pain and help it heal. Do you have questions for me?"

Avery managed a poor nod. "Was anyone else brought in with me?"

Dr Chaudhary placed his hand over Avery's arm to comfort her. "There was one other person in the house when the police arrived. They pronounced him dead at the scene. They brought you in alone."

Avery's face softened. "I'm safe now."

"You are safe here. A police officer stopped by yesterday to speak with you. I informed them you were not ready. He will more than likely drop by again sometime today for a statement when he hears you are awake. Now, I must do my rounds. Many patients to see this morning."

* * *

The realisation of what happened hit Avery like a brick, transporting her back to her bedroom. The belief that she would die that day, and the rage etched on Ethan's face as he pummelled her body with his enormous fists in a violent rage, would remain stamped in her memory. She recalled her jaw cracking beneath his powerful force. Panic consumed her while trying to fend him off, but Ethan was too strong. All she could do was protect her face and body by curling up into a ball to lessen the impact of his brutal force.

The pain was more excruciating with each blow. Avery thought he would never stop. She raised a hand to the back of her head, to find blood oozing. An image flashed before her of Nathan dragging her by the hair off the bed and onto the landing at the top of the staircase. Fear coursed through her like a surge of electricity as she realised Ethan's intentions. In that moment, it was her or him...

There was no escaping her last image: Ethan lying contorted and broken at the foot of the staircase. His eyes flickered while the remnants of life drained from his body. Avery focused on Ethan's eyes until they closed permanently. His body lay perfectly still. An image she would never forget. Relief gripped her, followed by intense guilt.

CHAPTER TWO

(Eighteen months ago)

*A*very glanced around her newly purchased two-bed house with immense pride. The panelled hallway and wooden flooring appealed to her aesthetic. She made a note to add a large industrial mirror above the modern radiator to finish the look at the entrance to her home. At twenty-eight years old, her long-awaited dream of owning her home was now a reality. It had taken five years and long working days to save for the deposit required to qualify for the mortgage. Owning her own home had been at the top of Avery's bucket list for as long as she could remember. It meant everything to her. Growing up, she never had a proper home. Her childhood had been transient.

Bounced from one children's home to another, because of an alcohol-fuelled, abusive mother, made Avery vulnerable and untrusting of people. Her mother's love was long since buried at the bottom of a thousand bottles. Memories of her childhood surfaced. Her seven-year-old self, furled in the corner of her sparse bedroom while her drunk mother entertained strangers she'd dragged home from the pub below. It always ended badly. Arguments followed by the smashing up of the house beneath her bedroom became the soundtrack to her childhood. Avery became accustomed to her mother leaving her home alone, too, but she never liked it. She found it even more unbearable as an only child suffering through each day and wishing that she had a sibling to navigate the misery with. But she didn't, forcing her to deal with the fallout of her mother's mistakes alone. She resented her mother, and the misery life forced her to deal with. The stench of stale alcohol permeated the air in the mornings, and Avery often navigated her mother's moods like a tightrope while preparing for school. Some mornings, she would wake up to her mother passed out on the couch half-dressed with an empty bottle of vodka strewn on the floor. Avery could not get out of the house fast enough.

It wasn't long before social services caught wind of Avery's neglectful mother through neighbours and the school she attended. The last image of her mother she remembered was passed out on the couch, holding an empty vodka bottle in one hand, and a burnt-out cigarette with a long stem of ash ready to fall in the other, while the social worker guided her through the living room and out of the house.

To this day, Avery has not seen her mother, and nor has her mother tried to reconnect with her. Avery had no desire to find her. She was free now, and looking back was not an option, promising herself to never talk about or reflect on her past. She would not be a victim of her circumstances. It was this mindset that helped her to navigate positively through life, once the decisions made about her life were in her hands and out of the state care system's control.

Avery worked hard after leaving the state care system to gain the qualifications needed to secure a role with her company, (Protecting Children Across Borders, or PCAB) which operated in over seventy-five countries. Outbound projects around the world and making a difference to others kept her going and gave her a purpose—a purpose she needed. It wasn't just for the children that she took the job; it was for herself, too. By helping the children, she was healing herself.

* * *

A knock at the door caught her attention. She ambled along the narrow hallway, opened the door, and smiled.

"Willow. What a surprise! Come in. I'm still getting organised. Navigate around the boxes."

Willow's mouth dropped open. "You did it, Avery! I am so proud of you. We must celebrate. How about going to Antonio's tonight, my treat?"

Avery looked around at the unpacked boxes. "I'm not sure. I still have so much to do."

Willow frowned. "I won't take no for an answer. The unpacking can wait. This achievement deserves a celebration, at least a toast."

Avery's mouth curled up. "Sure. Why not? I could do with a break."

"Great. I will book us a table now," she said, tapping on her phone while dodging the boxes into the kitchen.

Willow was her opposite in every way, Avery thought. She threw caution to the wind and took risks where she wouldn't. *Life was for living, not waiting,* Avery remembered her saying more than once. Willow lived in the moment and did not stress about the future.

She had had a picture-perfect upbringing with all the spoils. Nurturing loving parents and two siblings. A great education and childhood friends remained a constant in her life. Her 5.9-tall, slim frame towered above Avery's 5.5 feet. Willow's face was perfectly oval, dotted with freckles, and framed by insanely large eyelashes. Her beautiful, long auburn hair cascaded past her shoulders like a shot of fire. It revealed a mix of shimmering highlights under the sun's gaze. Willow had it all going on. The genuine beauty, though, lay beneath all of that. Willow always smiled and with a glass-half-full attitude towards any life struggles that happened to her.

Avery, on the other hand, was cautious, untrusting, and more comfortable in her own company than in large groups. A private person, her friends were composed of a small group of three and two of them were Willow and her brother Jackson. Willow was her closest confidant. But even Willow had a challenging time getting Avery to confide her past life to her. Jackson came close once following the premature death of his wife just over a year ago. To connect with Jackson during his darkest moments, Avery had revealed more than she felt comfortable with—although really, they were only small pockets of information here and there.

Willow and Jackson understood Avery in a way no one else did. They knew her need for privacy was important and respected her boundaries. They never pushed for more than Avery was willing to share. When all was said and done, Willow and Jackson knew little of Avery's past, only that it was painful for Avery to revisit. Occasionally, Avery would shut the world out, and her friends would not see her for a few days. However, they were used to their friend's dissociative behaviour and did not question it, knowing that it was probably a trauma response. Avery was who she was, and they accepted her for that.

She smiled recalling the day Jackson turned up unannounced at her rental apartment after hiding herself away for three days straight. *"I'm not taking no for an answer,"* he'd said. Holding up an old shabby picnic basket. *"Get your walking boots on, we're going to Woodberry creek for the day."* His patience and kindness brought her back into the world that day.

Avery picked up a small box and followed behind Willow. She placed it down on the countertop and began removing the contents and placing them in the cupboards while Willow booked a table at Antonio's restaurant.

"I'm on hold," Willow said, rolling her eyes. She tapped her phone to switch to speaker.

"This is what they have their customers listening to while they wait. Bloody awful music! I'm half tempted to hang up and book somewhere else," she moaned.

Avery laughed and continued to unpack the box. Her mobile phone vibrating on the table stopped her in her tracks. She noted

Jackson's number flashing across the top of the screen and smiled. "Hey, Jackson!"

"It's just a quick call to congratulate you on your new home. I know how much this means to you."

Avery heard baby Ruth crying in the background. Willow spun around and mouthed, "Who is it?"

"Jackson," she mouthed back.

"Avery, you still there?"

"I'm here."

"Sorry about that. Ruth tumbled over."

"Oh no. Is she okay?"

"Yeh, she's fine. Tough as nails, that one. Anyway, I must go. I will catch up with you next time I'm visiting my sisters. I'm proud of you, Avery. Bye for now."

Avery's smile reached her eyes as she tucked her phone into her jeans pocket.

Willow's eye's widened, and she flashed Avery a smile. "Yes, please, seven o'clock is great. My name is Willow Forbes. Thank you," Willow finished.

She turned to Avery. "We're all booked in. How's Jackson?"

"He just wanted to congratulate me on all this," said Avery holding her arms up and spinning around!"

Willow raised her brow mischievously.

"What?" pressed Avery.

"Nothing. Nothing at all," she teased.

"I'm going to dash. My hair appointment is at noon. I will pick you up at around 6:45."

"Sounds good to me. I'll be ready. Let yourself out. See you later."

Avery smiled as she went from box to box, recalling the day that she first had met Willow. Juggling a tray of drinks, Avery struggled to navigate around a group of drunk college students at the Red Herring Club in the town centre. It was her first night, and it wasn't going well. Willow appeared just in time to avert a disaster and caught the tray as Avery slipped.

"That was close!" laughed Willow.

"Thank you. I'm Avery."

"And you can call me Willow," she beamed.

Moving to the small town of Cotswood offered Avery a fresh start and exuded old-world charm, and meeting Willow made it even more special. This carefree interlude was the beginning of a longstanding friendship. She warmed to Willow instantly. From that day on, they became firm friends. Willow was the light Avery needed in her life. Loyal, kind, and honest. Willow was the most genuine person Avery had ever met. That was six years ago when they were working night shifts at the club while waiting for call-backs or rejections on job applications after graduating from university. Graduates saturated the job market and there were few openings locally. The bar job was a temporary steppingstone that brought them together.

The youngest of two siblings, one sister and one brother. Willow's parents were liberal to an extent and encouraged rather than prevented her carefree personality, allowing her to be her true self without hindrance. And Avery witnessed first-hand the benefits of this great, unstifled relationship. The love between them was clear for all to see. And Avery could only have dreamed of such a loving family growing up.

CHAPTER THREE

*W*illow parked outside Antonio's restaurant and climbed out, followed by Avery.

"I'm starving," Willow blurted, pushing open the door to the restaurant.

"Me too. It just occurred to me I haven't eaten since breakfast." Avery stumbled on her heels. Willow giggled. "Every time, Avery!"

Avery rolled her eyes. "Seriously, I don't know why I bother. Give me my old faithful Docs any day. These damn things are torture."

The Maître d', a grumpy man with an attitude, led them to their reserved table, then returned to the booking desk without pulling out their chairs.

"This is perfect," Willow commented as she sat down.

"But they seriously need to reconsider the frontman for this place. Did you see the miserable look on his face?"

"Maybe he's having a bad day?"

"Oh, come on, he's just a sour face!"

Avery glanced out of the window and smiled. "This is lovely."

Willow's face lit up when she noticed three men enter. "Now

that is my kind of man!" She watched them as they were directed to their table.

Avery barely glanced at them while Willow's eyes fixed on the guy at the back. "I think I'm in love!" gushed Willow. "Oh God, he just looked over!"

Willow snapped her head back and focused on her wineglass. "Is he still looking?"

Avery discreetly glanced over. "Yep. He's looking right at ya with a beaming smile. Now let's order, I'm starving."

"Food. Yes. Good idea."

Avery laughed. Willow was a breath of fresh air. She oozed confidence, and Avery admired that. They both glanced over the menus and once they'd decided, Willow beckoned over the waiter.

"You ready to order?"

"Yes," nodded Willow. "Can I have the halloumi salad to start and the carbonara for the main, please?" she turned to Avery. "I need carbs and calories today!"

The waiter nodded and jotted down Willow's order.

He glanced over at Avery. "I will have the same, please."

"Would you like a table wine to accompany your meal?"

"No, thank you. I'm driving," advised Willow, she looked at Avery. "There's nothing stopping you having some wine?"

Avery turned to the waiter. "Not for me, thanks."

"Your order will be around fifteen minutes," the waiter informed.

"Thank you," acknowledged Avery as the waiter turned on his heel and headed to the three men seated at four tables in front of them.

Willow looked over her shoulder briefly. The man she was so enamoured with glanced back and offered a cheeky smile.

"He's cute," she flustered.

Avery's eyes connected with the tallest of the men sitting facing directly in her line of vision. She drew her eyes away and began fumbling with the menu.

"What are you doing?" pressed Willow, puzzled.

"Nothing. Why?"

"You're all flustered."

"No, I'm not."

"You are so, Avery Masters!"

Willow, again, glanced over her shoulders and noted the reason for Avery's flustering.

"Ah. I get it now! He's too handsome for his own good, that one. He likes you, it seems."

"Well, I am not interested. I just want to enjoy a meal with my friend and nothing more," insisted Avery.

"You are far too serious. Relax a little and enjoy the attention. What harm could a little flirting do?"

"You know I'm no good at that sort of thing."

"Okay, then at least smile back at him."

The waiter approached with their order and organised their plates on the table. He placed a bowl of garlic bread in the centre. "Enjoy your meal, ladies."

Avery smiled. "Thank you."

Five minutes later, the waiter appeared with a bottle of expensive wine. "From the gentleman on table five." He glanced over his shoulder to show the table.

Willow turned around, smiled, and mouthed thank you to the man who caught her eye earlier.

"Can we take this home? I'm driving."

"Works for me!" agreed Avery.

"This is amazing. I might try to replicate this dish at home one weekend," commented Avery.

"Make sure I'm over when you do!"

"Of course," Avery agreed, wrangling a sliver of pasta.

"How's your sister?"

Willow rolled her eyes. "Lucy is a pain in the ass, as always. Constantly in my closet. She drives me insane. Half my clothes are strewn across her bedroom floor."

"So, no change there, then. When are your parents due over from Spain?"

"Strange you ask. They are coming to England next month for a wedding. Lucy and I are flying over to see them for their anniversary in a couple of months, too. You should come with us."

"I can't. I will be in Africa."

"Of course, you will. Maybe next time."

After they finished their meal, the waiter cleared their table and brought over the dessert menu. Willow shook her head. "I couldn't eat anything else, so not for me. Thank you."

Avery shook her head. "Same for me. No thanks."

The waiter closed the dessert menu. "Would you like the bill?"

Willow glanced at Avery and then shot a glance at table five. "Let's stay for five or ten minutes, pretty please?"

Avery rolled her eyes. "Sure!"

Avery turned to the waiter. "Not yet. Can we order two coffees, please?"

The waiter forced a smile and headed to the kitchen.

The guy from table five who'd been eyeing Willow stood up and headed over to their table.

"Willow, don't look now, but that guy is walking over here!"

"Seriously?"

Before Avery could answer, he was at the table. His dark thick hair and tall muscular frame was not lost on Willow.

"Hi, I hope you don't mind the intrusion. I just wanted to give you my number." He handed a card to Willow. She glanced at the name. "Hi, Dillon. I'm Willow."

Dillon could not take his eyes off her. "Willow," he repeated. "I look forward to your call," he smiled and then walked back to his table.

Willow could barely contain herself. "OMG," she mouthed to Avery,"

"Willow Forbes, you never cease to amaze me!"

The waiter brought their coffee.

"Thank you," Willow smiled.

They drank their coffee, paid the bill, and made to leave. As they passed by table five, one of Dillon's group stood up, blocking Avery's path. "Hi, can I ask your name?"

Avery paused and then, remembering what Willow said at the table earlier, she offered a smile. "Avery."

"Avery. An unusual but beautiful name. Can I take your number?"

Avery's eyes shifted to Willow. Willow's lips curled. She nodded her head, encouraging Avery to say yes.

"Sure."

"My name is Ethan, by the way." He retrieved his phone from his pocket. "Okay, what's your number?" Avery gave her number and Ethan added it to his contacts. "It was lovely to meet you, Avery." The dulcet tone of his voice echoed through Avery's body. Her face flushed, and she turned away from him, embarrassed that he may have noticed. Avery and Willow headed out of Antonio's and straight to the car.

"Wow! He is something else. Did you hear that voice?" gushed Willow.

"I know, right?"

"I bet Ethan calls you tomorrow. He is smitten with you. It's written all over his face. The way he seemed to look straight into the depths of your soul with those gorgeous eyes sent tingles down my spine!"

Avery rolled her eyes. "You are so dramatic!"

"Not dramatic, simply romantic. Something you need more of in your life, Avery Masters."

Avery belted up and glanced out of the car window, straight through the restaurant window. Ethan was looking straight at her, and their eyes locked briefly.

"Avery, did you hear me?" prompted Willow, interrupting her thoughts.

"Sorry, what?"

Willow raised a brow. "I said, do you want to come back to my house, or do you want to go straight home?"

"Straight home. I want to have a bath. I'm tired."

"No problem. Now, hear me out. If Ethan calls, say yes to a date. Don't brush him off and make excuses why you can't, like you did the last time a guy was interested. It will be good for you to date and have some fun. And I haven't seen too many guys like Ethan around Cotswood for some time!"

Avery simply nodded and unclipped her seat belt as they approached her drive. Willow reached over and kissed her on the cheek. "I'll call you tomorrow after work. Message me if Ethan calls, okay?"

"You will be the first to know, I promise." Avery climbed out of the car. Willow beeped her horn and drove off. Avery watched the taillights disappear out of sight and then ambled into her house, locking the door behind her.

CHAPTER FOUR

*H*ammering on her door jolted Avery awake. "What the hell..." she cursed while reaching for her robe. She hurried downstairs to answer the door.

"Parcel for Miss Masters. Sign here, please?" greeted the postman.

Avery signed the digital box and took the large parcel. "Thank you." After closing the door, she put the parcel on the countertop. After starting the coffee machine and opening the blinds, she sat at the kitchen table to open her parcel. Avery peeked inside and saw that it was the large wall art that she ordered a few days earlier. She lay the box flat on the table and slid out the heavy frame and gasped. *Wow!* The 80 x 80-centimetre framed poem, *IF*, by Rudyard Kipling stunned her. *It will look incredible in the dining room. Another great purchase from Etsy,* she mused. She placed it back in the box. Her mobile phone ringing caught her off guard–*Ethan!*

Her heart raced while swiping to answer.

"Hi, it's Ethan."

"Hi," answered Avery, surprised.

"I hope it's not too soon. Would you like to go to dinner on Saturday?"

Avery fell silent. She wasn't expecting him to call so soon. Regardless of Willow's confidence that he would.

"Hello. You still there?" pressed Ethan.

"Yes, sorry. You surprised me, that's all."

"So, about dinner on Saturday?"

"Yes, sure."

"Great. I will pick you up at seven if that works for you?"

"Seven is good. I will ping you my address."

"I look forward to it," finished Ethan.

Avery stared at her phone in disbelief. Feeling unsure that she was doing the right thing, she called Willow for reassurance.

"Willow, sorry to call you at work. Have you got time to talk?"

"Sure, make it quick. I have a meeting in five minutes."

"Ethan called!"

"Wow! He's eager. I told you he would. Please tell me you agreed to see him?"

"Yes, this coming Saturday. He's taking me to dinner."

"That's great. So, why do you sound like you were just invited to a funeral?"

"I'm just not sure it's what I want. I've just bought my house and work is sending me to Africa in two weeks. It's bad timing to get into something new, don't you think?"

"Now, listen to me, Avery Masters. There isn't a perfect time to start a relationship with a guy. If it's meant to be, it will work, and if not, then what the hell do you have to lose? If nothing else, you will enjoy a nice meal with an insanely good-looking guy. It's not a win-or-lose situation, it's just dinner at this point. Then you can decide if you want to see him again. You're overthinking it."

"You're right, of course. I always do this. I feel better about it already."

"That's my girl. I must go. My manager is throwing me daggers from across the room! I'll call you later."

. . .

Avery picked up where she had left off the night before. Surrounded by boxes, she pulled the one closest and emptied the contents onto the floor. Her heart skipped a beat when her eyes rested on her childhood journal. A chill ran the length of her spine. She hadn't seen it for years. She drew a deep breath, sat against the living room wall, and opened it.

She turned the pages and stopped on a highlighted entry. A familiar feeling washed over her—fear. She turned away and placed the journal on the floor. "I can't. I just can't," she said aloud. She sighed. *Come on Avery, you can do this. You must face it or throw the damn book out once and for all,* she convinced herself. She picked the journal up off the floor and began to read.

December 14th

The worst birthday ever! I'm ten today. Mum keeps screaming at me. Not sure why. She's locked me in my room again. She nailed the window shut so I can't open it. I just want to die. I'm scared. I don't want to live like this anymore. She's drunk again. I can hear strangers below. They scare me. There's lots of shouting, swearing and the music is loud. Someone tried to open my bedroom door again. Once they realised it was locked, they stopped. This happens often, too.

I have a test at school tomorrow. I asked mum to help me practise, but she was too busy with her visitors. Instead, she yelled and screamed, ordering me to my room and then locked me in to ensure I would not come downstairs and ruin her night.

I think she forgot it's my birthday. No mention of it. No card this year. Not even a happy birthday. I feel so alone. I hate birthdays. Just another reminder that I am worthless, living in a world I hate, with a mother who barely knows I exist anymore.

I see a lone magpie sitting on the window ledge outside my room. It comes often. Mum once told me seeing just one of them is bad luck. I see this magpie often. I think mum's right.

Avery was about to close her journal when a piece of paper fell out. She picked it up, turned it over and let out a woeful breath. It was a poem. One she'd written. A memory surfaced. She recalled the night clearly. Her mother had locked her in her room again. Confused and defeated, she sat in the corner of her room and poured her feelings onto this yellowed piece of scrap paper from an old notebook.

She held it up and read it:

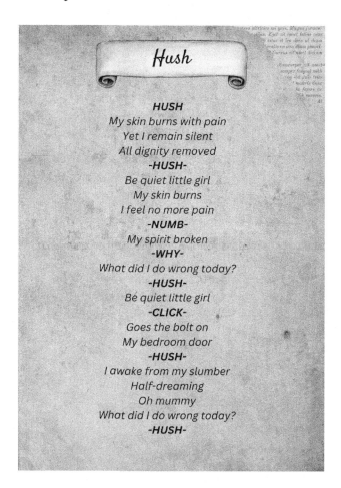

HUSH
My skin burns with pain
Yet I remain silent
All dignity removed
-HUSH-
Be quiet little girl
My skin burns
I feel no more pain
-NUMB-
My spirit broken
-WHY-
What did I do wrong today?
-HUSH-
Be quiet little girl
-CLICK-
Goes the bolt on
My bedroom door
-HUSH-
I awake from my slumber
Half-dreaming
Oh mummy
What did I do wrong today?
-HUSH-

She slipped the piece of paper between the pages of her journal, closed it, and placed it back in the box. The image of the magpie on her window ledge tormented her. She swiped a tear from her cheek and wrapped her arms around her torso. *You're not a child anymore, Avery. You control your life now. Leave all that pain in the past.* She sighed. *Mum can't hurt me anymore. I control my destiny now,* she repeated. She fought hard to prevent herself from sinking low and ruining her day. Something she had mastered well over the years. It was a battle sometimes lost—but not today. She leapt to her feet and continued working her way through the remaining boxes until they were all done.

She stood back with pride once she had found a home for everything, and she could see her living room floor again. Avery retrieved her new artwork and hung it in the centre of the dining room wall. She stood back and admired it. *Perfect!*

At the end of the day, feeling proud of herself, she opened the fridge and glanced at the bottle of wine the guys had gifted her and Willow at the restaurant. *Not that one, Willow would never forgive me!* She reached for the cheaper bottle she'd bought from Asda, poured herself a large glass, and slumped down on her sofa, losing herself in her thoughts. *I can't believe I did it. I bought my home! And it feels amazing. I am right where I need to be. No one will ever take my freedom away from me again. A proper home, my safe space.*

Her mobile phone ringing thrust her from her thoughts. She glanced at her phone and saw Willow's number flashing across the screen.

"Hey."

"I have had the worst day!" revealed Willow.

"What happened?"

"Remember earlier, I mentioned I had a meeting?"

Avery chimed in. "Yes, I remember."

"Well, after the meeting, I pulled my boss aside and pitched an idea to her, and she directly shut me down. However, later in the day, I was passing by her office. She was on a call to head office—

her boss—and I overheard her pitching the same idea that I had just pitched to her. It was the same idea with a few tweaks, Avery! I am so angry with her. The audacity of the woman." Willow paused.

Avery spoke up. "I don't know what to say. Have you tried talking to her?"

"You're kidding, right? The woman is a top-grade bitch. She would probably find a reason to fire me. I heard rumours in the past that she would often take credit for other people's ideas, but I had never witnessed it first-hand. Until now, they were just office rumours. I've had enough of this job. I can no longer work for someone like her. She will never allow me to progress within the company. It's not the first time she has waved off my ideas, but I just thought they were not good enough. For all I know, she pitched them to her boss, too." Willow took a breath. Whenever she was frustrated, she talked at top speed.

"Other than confronting your boss, which I'm guessing you won't do, my advice is to look for a company that will value you. You deserve better than this, Willow." Avery could hear Willow choking up in the background.

"Why don't you come over to my place, stay the night, and go to work from here in the morning?" Avery suggested. "We can talk it through over a glass of wine or two?"

"That sounds perfect. I will be there in under an hour. Just need to have a quick bath and pack an overnight bag. See you shortly."

Avery placed her phone on the coffee table and finished her glass of wine. Then went to the kitchen to prepare comfort food for Willow. An easy pasta bake she used to rustle up in their younger days when they both worked at the club.

Avery made a quick change into her loungewear and placed the box with her childhood journal into the cabinet, not wanting Willow to see it. No one had seen it and she wanted to keep it that way. She made a mental note to haul it up to the loft when she had some spare time.

It wasn't long before Willow was rapping on the front door. Avery greeted her with a hug.

"I needed that. Thanks. Now a large glass of wine is in order! Let's crack open that ridiculously expensive wine those guys bought us."

Willow followed Avery into the kitchen, and her nose twitched. "Mmm, something smells familiar."

Avery smiled and headed over to the oven, popped on her oven gloves, and retrieved the pasta bake. "Surprise!"

"And that is why you are my best friend. You always know the perfect way to cheer me up. Gosh, your pasta bake has seen us through some tough times. You know, Avery, this dish is tied to so many happy memories. Thanks for cooking this tonight."

"Hey, it was nothing. I just wanted to cheer you up and I know how much you love this dish."

Willow headed to the cupboards and began opening them one by one. "Where do you keep your plates?"

"We can eat in here; hell, why bother with plates?" Avery said as she carried the pasta dish to the living room and placed it on the coffee table. "Let's just dig in."

"Like the old days, hey! Remember when we would get back late from working for the club and we would get two spoons and wolf down a large bowl of this that you'd prepared earlier in the day for when our shift was over," recalled Willow diving into the pasta first.

"Yeh, and we would watch reruns of *Friends* until we fell asleep. Good times," recalled Avery, wrangling with a sliver of pasta.

"I never did understand your obsession with Ross!"

Avery poked Willow in the arm. "Oh, come on, your obsession with Chandler was far worse."

"What are you talking about? Chandler was hilarious."

"True. But Ross was adorable."

"Nope. Still don't see it!"

Avery put her fork down. "What are you going to do about work?"

Willow shook her head. "Truthfully, I don't know. I just know I can't continue working for my company. It's sucking the life out of me. Changing career paths is something that I'm thinking about. I want to do something more satisfying and freer. I'm thinking of going freelance, setting up my own website and taking it from there. I have made a bunch of contacts over the last two years. I know they will put the word out for me."

"With your graphic design and web design skills, your multi-talents will carry you far. I love the idea. And besides, more people are taking the plunge, leaving their nine-to-fives, and setting up on their own."

"Thanks for always supporting me. I don't know what I'd do without you."

"On to lighter things. Have you called Dillon yet?"

"Not yet. I thought I'd leave it for a couple of days. Keep him waiting."

Avery shook her head mockingly. "You are so bad!"

"Yep. I like to play hard to get. Keeps things interesting."

Avery picked up the bottle of wine and topped up their glasses. They talked until the early hours and eventually fell asleep head-to-toe on the large sofa.

CHAPTER FIVE

*S*aturday arrived and Avery battled with her nerves. She drank the last of her matcha smoothie and headed upstairs to her bedroom. The hinge on her wardrobe was stiff. She tugged at the door, almost toppling backwards. Huffing, she regained her composure and opened the door wider. She rifled through the closet rails until her fingers rested on a white cotton summer dress. *Perfect, understated, and classic,* she mused. Continuing her search at the back of her closet, Avery reached for her nude strappy sandals and then held the dress against her body and studied her reflection in the large free-standing mirror.

"That will do," she said aloud. Then headed for the shower to freshen up.

Avery pressed both hands flat against the tiled wall while the warm water cascaded over the deep scars on her back. She reached around to her back and ran her finger over the deepest scar. *Your life is in your hands now, Avery. Just keep reminding yourself of that.*

After showering, Avery sat at the dressing table and applied her make-up, ensuring that she kept it light and fresh for a barely-there look. Her favoured look for summer. It was warm outside, and the nights were light, not getting dark until around ten in the evening. She forked her fingers through her hair and sighed. *What to do with this?* She procrastinated. *Straight–I shall wear it straight. It's decided.* She pulled open her large bottom drawer that was home to all her hair care products and reached for her straighteners and began perfecting her sleek, classy look for the evening. Once complete, she stood in front of the mirror and glanced over her lithe, toned reflection for a few moments. Her lips curved up, barely recognising herself from earlier in the day. *Not bad, Avery, not bad at all.* It was almost seven, and she felt anxious. Butterflies circled her stomach. *I need a glass of wine!* She hurried downstairs to the kitchen, retrieved the half-empty bottle of wine from the fridge and poured herself a glass, then drank it in one gulp.

Okay, Avery, you can do this. It's just a date, for goodness' sake. The doorbell startled her. *Oh God, he's here!* She paused, inhaled a deep breath, popped a mint in her mouth, and headed for the door.

Ethan stood before her looking incredibly handsome in a crisp white shirt with the top button undone, teamed with a black semi-fitted suit jacket left open and tight matching trousers that accentuated his sculpted thighs. Her heart skipped a beat. His dark, thick hair brushed off his face effortlessly and his green eyes sparkled.

Ethan's smile reached his eyes. "You look incredible," he commented, barely able to take his eyes off her.

"Thank you," blushed Avery.

Ethan extended his hand. "Shall we?"

Avery locked the door and walked alongside Ethan to his car. A black Range Rover, which had clearly been through the car wash for the occasion. Ethan held open the passenger door for her.

"I hope you like surprises!"

Avery's eyes widened.

"Don't worry. You will love what I have planned for the evening," Ethan assured.

Ethan pulled off the driveway and took a left. His window wound half-down, encouraged a gentle breeze that lifted his scent and wafted past Avery's nose. She breathed it in, delighting in the fresh summer aroma. She side-glanced to look him over. His toned arms and large hands caught her attention. Her lips curled, and she caught herself blushing. Ethan turned and smiled, then re-focused his attention on the road ahead.

"Not long now," he advised.

A look of curiosity crossed Avery's face. "Where is it we're going?"

"If I told you, it wouldn't be a surprise!"

Ethan turned down a lonely country road. Avery didn't recognise the route. Ethan continued down the narrow lane for a further fifteen minutes and then took a sharp left, pulled into a clearing and parked up. Avery scanned the immediate area, greeted by blooming wildflower-filled meadows and the glistening shimmer of a lake in the distance. The sun was getting low, and the lake was adorned with glitter sparkles under the sun's gaze.

Puzzled, she turned to him. "I'm confused. Where is it you're taking me, exactly?"

Ethan remained silent. He got out of the car, walked to the passenger side, and opened the door. He extended his hand and Avery placed her hand in his.

"We have a bit of a walk, but trust me, it will be worth it!" he assured, keeping the details of the date close to his chest.

Avery glanced down at her feet and took off her sandals, and to make her feel more comfortable, Ethan removed his shoes. Avery's smile reached up to the corner of her eyes. She found Ethan intoxicating and wondered why he was single.

He laced his fingers through Avery's and led her across the meadow to the lake. The feel of their fingers entwined sent tingles rushing through her body.

"Wow! I never knew this was here. It's beautiful."

Ethan glanced at Avery and saw the delight on her face. "We are almost there. Just a few more minutes."

They walked around to the far side of the lake. When Ethan stopped, Avery's eyes widened. "Seriously! You did all of this?"

"Well, as much as I would love to take the credit, I can't. I hired a company that specialises in dream dates! Yes, it's a thing—who knew, hey! I wanted our first date to be special. A friend of mine put me onto the company that organised this for us."

Avery's eyes trailed over the beautiful gazebo covered in string lights. The white flowy drapes stirred in the gentle summer breeze. Centred in the gazebo were a beautifully dressed table and two chairs. In front of the gazebo, a little closer to the lake's edge was a perfectly positioned double lounger covered in gorgeous scatter cushions. Solar flame lights glimmered casting a warm glow. Ethan caught Avery glancing at the lounger.

"Now that is for star gazing, glancing out onto the lake, and talking into the early hours. Purely to get to know one another, I promise," he reassured.

"I, erm, I was not worried!" she blushed until her cheeks felt like they were going to drop off.

Ethan pulled a box from a large chest at the back of the gazebo. He pulled out a large, chequered blanket, champagne, and a summer picnic prepared by a professional chef. Avery watched as Ethan placed napkins and placemats on the table, corked the champagne and laid out the cutlery, plates, canapés, finger food, and champagne flutes.

Avery was in awe of Ethan. She studied his face, which radiated a warm glow from the setting sun peeking through the drapes. *His sharp chiselled jawline would not look out of place on the cover of a magazine,* she thought. But it was his deep green eyes that captivated her most of all. She watched as he forked his fingers through his thick raven hair, swept back off his face, with just a slither sloping his forehead.

"Thank you for doing this. It's perfect. I'm blown away by all your effort. It's so unexpected."

"A friend of mine once told me if you're not prepared to impress a first date, then it does not bode well for the relationship ahead. The thing is, until now, I've never been inspired enough to go to this length."

"Your friend sounds like a wise man!"

Ethan pulled out a chair. Avery delicately adjusted herself in the seat and watched Ethan organise the table. He held two champagne flutes between his fingers, poured the champagne expertly and offered her one. As she took the flute, his fingers brushed against hers, and her stomach flip-flopped. He looked into her eyes and held his gaze for a moment before toasting. Holding up his glass, he toasted, "To new beginnings."

Avery tilted her glass. "To new beginnings."

Ethan lightly filled his plate and ate. Avery cherry-picked the lighter canapes and popped one in her mouth. "Mmm! These are incredible. Kudos to the chef!"

Ethan nodded in agreement. "He is one of the best in our town." He paused, wiped his hands with a napkin, and took a sip of his drink before continuing. "I want to know more about you. So, tell me, who is Avery Masters?"

Avery leaned back in her chair, sipping intermittently. "There's not much to know. I have no family to speak of. My mother and I are estranged. I worked hard to put myself through university. I was lucky enough to meet Willow, my closest and most trusted friend. To be honest, I keep my circle of friends small. I'd rather have two or three genuine friends than a catalogue of acquaintances who purport to be friends and run a mile when you truly need them. I just bought my first house, a small two-bed, and it's simply perfect for me. I am private and don't showcase my life on social media, a trend that has never made sense to me. We are all different, I guess."

Ethan studied Avery for the longest time. She turned away from his gaze, embarrassed.

"I'm sorry. I didn't mean to make you feel uncomfortable. If you don't mind me saying, you are stunningly beautiful. The moment I walked into the restaurant and saw you sitting at the table, you enamoured me. You have a look of vulnerability about you, though. I couldn't help but notice you looked like you did not want to be there."

"How on earth did you pick up on that from the first glance? You're right though. Willow encouraged me out of the house. It was her idea of a celebration of my becoming a homeowner. Still, I enjoyed it. If it were not for Willow, I would barely leave the house. My home is my comfort zone. I like my own company and just don't need to be around people all the time. Willow is the opposite of me, a social bunny and adventurer. Nothing fazes her at all, and she fears nothing. I wish I were more like her. I am getting better at the whole socialising thing. But it requires a lot of effort on my part."

Ethan picked up the bottle of champagne and refilled their glasses. "And what is it you do for work?" he asked.

"I work for an international children's charity, PCAB. You may have heard of them."

Ethan interjected, "Yes, of course. It's well known for the work they do for orphans and vulnerable families around the world. I'm impressed. Tell me more."

"I love what I do. I am a project manager. My job takes me all over the world for two months at a time. We help give children and families a better life. Rebuilding villages, installing running water and so on. It's extremely rewarding. We need to find a refuge for families who are victims of war-torn environments. These families lose everything and flee their towns with nothing more than what they are wearing on their backs. We help them rebuild their lives and provide safe shelter to get them back on their feet and independent again. My colleagues and I work on a rota basis, two months on and two months off during peak times. I am currently on a two-month break that ends in a fortnight."

Ethan displayed a forlorn look on his face. He took a sip from his glass and then placed it down on the table. "Well then, we better make the next two weeks count!"

"Assuming there will be a second date," Avery teased.

Ethan's green eyes sparkled. "Avery Masters, would you do me the honour of accompanying me on a second date?" The corners of Ethan's mouth turned up.

Happiness glowed inside of her. "Of course, Mr? Ah, it occurs to me I don't know your surname?"

"It's Channing—Ethan Channing."

"Channing. Mmm, I like that," commented Avery.

"It's of English origin, and 'Channing' means 'young wolf.' So, there you have it."

"Well, I'd better be careful then!" teased Avery.

Ethan's eyes drew together momentarily. "Well, wolves are notoriously territorial and prefer just one mate for life. Not an undesirable trait to have, in my humble opinion. But what do I know? I am merely human!" Ethan smiled, playfully shrugging his shoulders.

He continued. "Shall we take our glasses over to the lounger? The sunset is almost complete, and we wouldn't want to miss it."

Avery stood up. "I would love to."

They picked up their glasses and sat side by side on the oversized lounger. The setting sun cast a beautiful orange glow across the lake. The night sky was clear. A flock of Canada geese grouped on the far side of the lake, settling down for the evening. Tall reeds provided shelter for the ducks and nesting swans. Birds rustled in nearby trees as they took cover for the night. The gentle night breeze brought the fragrance of wildflowers passed Avery's nose. She took a deep breath and lay her head against the oversized cushions.

"This is my heaven. It's beautiful here. Thank you for bringing me. This is perfect."

Ethan inched closer and took Avery's hand, lacing his fingers through hers. The perfect gentleman. He did not make a move on Avery, no awkward kiss, and no corny lines. Ethan relaxed his head on the cushion, and they shared a comfortable silence observing the last of the disappearing sunset. The moon took over, illuminating the night sky and the world below.

Avery turned to Ethan. "I would like to know more about you. So, who is Ethan Channing, the young wolf?"

Ethan searched Avery's eyes intoxicated by her. "Ethan Channing is a young man taken with a young, mysterious woman called Avery Masters."

Avery did not avert her gaze this time. She held her position and leaned in, surprising herself. Ethan met her halfway and their lips touched for the first time.

Avery felt Ethan's rapid heartbeat...his lips were soft...she did not want the night to end.

They talked into the early hours of Sunday morning. Ethan couldn't take his eyes off her. Avery's glass-like skin and long sleek hair blowing in the evening breeze, took his breath away.

"I guess we should head back," Ethan suggested.

Avery nodded, feeling a little sad her date was ending. Surprising herself, considering she was not enthused about a date with Ethan, to begin with. Now she did not want it to end.

"So, what will happen with all this stuff?"

"Don't worry about that. I just need to drop the company a message to let them know we have left. They send their team to clear it all. I think it's a genius concept, simple and yet perfect. I cannot believe it has not been a thing before now."

"I agree. It has been a unique date for sure. Certainly, a first for me. Thank you."

They picked up their shoes and strolled across the dark meadow. Ethan laced his fingers through Avery's as they headed back to the car. The feel of Ethan's hands wrapped around hers as they strolled through the meadow filled her pounding heart with happiness. Ethan enamoured Avery, too. He had been the perfect gentleman throughout the evening, assuming nothing. He took the night at her pace and respected the silent boundaries she set. She'd met no one like him. She felt as if he understood her perfectly.

They climbed into the car. Ethan paused and turned to Avery before starting the engine, searching her face, before leaning in. She met him halfway and for the second time that evening, their lips met, and the softness of his lips mirrored Avery's.

"I just had to do that one more time before I took you home." He turned his attention to the road ahead and pulled away from the clearing.

Avery glanced out of the window and occasionally stole a glance Ethan's way, taking in his silhouette. He looked back, displaying a warm, genuine smile, and continued driving. The comfortable silence between them was powerful and breath-taking, and she felt it strongly, unlike anything else she'd experienced in her life. She savoured the moment.

CHAPTER SIX

S unday morning, Avery rose after ten. She glanced at her
phone and shot out of bed. "Oh, no!"

Willow had called three times. Avery called her straight back.

"Finally! I'm guessing you had a late night."

"Yes, I did! And it was amazing, Willow."

"Well, pray tell. Don't hold back. Spill!"

"It was the perfect date. Ethan organised our date through a
company called Dream Dates. Have you heard of them before?"

"Never. But I want to know more," pushed Willow.

Avery described the evening. "I hate to think how much it cost
him to organise. A top chef prepared the picnic. It was like a scene
from a movie. No exaggeration."

"Oh, Avery, I am so happy for you. No one has ever gone to that
much trouble for me. I need to up my game! I am seriously jealous.
He sounds perfect for you. So, when are you seeing him again?"

"Tonight!"

"Really?"

"Yep! I think I'm smitten, Willow. No one has ever made me

feel this way before. It's like he could see me, and I mean really see me. I've met no one like him. I never believed men like Ethan existed."

Willow gasped. "Well, he certainly exists, and you have a second date tonight. You deserve this. It's been a long time coming. Now for the important stuff: did you kiss?"

"Of course! And that's all we did before you probe further."

Willow laughed down the phone. "You know me too well, Avery Masters."

"So, I won't be seeing you today then," Willow continued. "How about tomorrow after work? I have decided to hand in my notice. I will need to talk about it over a large bottle of wine, and I need you to tell me how I did the right thing!"

"Seriously? That's brilliant news. I'm proud of you. Yes, come over tomorrow and tell me all about it. Exciting times. And yes, you are doing the right thing. So don't give it another thought."

"Exiting times for both of us."

"Have you called Dillon yet?" Avery pressed.

"Yes. I called him this morning. He seems keen. We are meeting up on Wednesday evening for dinner."

"I can't wait to hear all about it."

Willow chimed in. "Don't worry, I will give you the complete lowdown! I will see you tomorrow after six."

Avery put her mobile phone on charge and then ran a bath to prepare for her date later. Visions of the night before took up pole position in her mind. Lying back in the warm water, she closed her eyes and relived every second of the night. Later while drying off, she saw her reflection in the mirror and turned to the side. She winced at the sight of the deep scars embedded in her back. Her mood dropped and worry took over. The thought of a man seeing her naked scared her. *The moment will come, and I will have to bare all! I need to tell Ethan about my scars. It's only fair to warn him. Then the ball is in his court.* She turned away from the mirror.

* * *

Ethan sat down at his breakfast bar and googled Avery Masters. He wanted to know more about the woman who had captured his heart. His search revealed little to his disappointment. *She was right. Social media is not her thing, which is refreshing,* he mused. The only thing Google brought up was her job at PCAB. He clicked on her company's profile image and read about her accomplishments with the company. Impressed, he realised Avery wasn't like most women. She was different.

Ethan's mobile phone interrupted his thoughts. He glanced at his brother's number flashing across the top of the screen and answered.

"Hey, Damian, what do I owe the pleasure?"

"Hey bro, just a quick catch-up. Killing some time before I head off to Peru for a month. How are you doing?"

"I'm good. I met someone. She's called, Avery."

Damian fell silent.

"Damian, are you still there?"

"Yeh, sorry. Is it serious?"

"We've only been on one date. Seeing her again tonight. She's incredible, different from anyone I have met before."

"I've heard that before. As your big brother, it is my job to impart worthy advice. Take it slow this time, bro. Don't dive in too fast. Enjoy the journey. Less intensity. You know how you get."

"I don't know what you're talking about, Damian."

"Sure, you do. If this Avery girl is so incredible, then slow and steady wins the race. Let her lead the way and don't take over. I'm just saying for your own good. You can be intense, bro. Just remember what happened the last time. It didn't end well."

"Right. Gotchya. Thanks for the reminder. Anyhow, I must go. Hope all is well down under. Maybe I will come to visit you in Australia later this year. No promises, though. Enjoy Peru."

Rattled by his brother's unwanted advice, Ethan brought the call to a swift end and threw his phone down on the sofa. *He has no idea what he's talking about. Maybe once he has secured a successful long-standing relationship himself, he will be better equipped to dish out advice on matters of relationships.*

CHAPTER SEVEN

*E*than arrived promptly and beeped his horn. Avery grabbed her handbag and hurried outside.

Ethan cast his eyes over Avery approvingly, a vision of classic beauty that took his breath away. Barely able to contain his joy, he climbed out of his car, walked around to the passenger side, and opened the door for her.

"Thank you," she said while climbing in. She caught his distinctive aroma of Dior Sauvage, teasing her senses as Ethan closed the passenger door. She inhaled slowly, delighting in his scent. He hurried around to the driver's side and hopped in. Avery turned to him, observing the dimple in his chin and his sharp, striking jawline.

"What is it?" Ethan asked.

Avery fiddled with her seatbelt nervously. "Nothing," she smiled, finally clipping in the stubborn belt.

"And where are we going this evening?"

"It would be hard to top last night. However, I don't think you will be disappointed."

Ethan headed towards town. Avery stole another glance at

Ethan while he drove. Butterflies circled her stomach just like the night before. She couldn't remember the last time she felt this happy. Ethan glanced at her. His eyes intense as he searched her face. His lips curled. She noted the crease on the side of his nose and the genuine smile that reached his eyes. Her heart skipped a beat, and she placed her hand over her chest.

"We're almost there." He pulled up and parked behind an old ruin. Avery's eyes trailed over her surroundings. Puzzled, she turned to Ethan. "Where are we?"

"You are going to have to trust me again!"

They climbed out of the car, and Ethan took Avery's hand and led her down a cobbled path towards the outer bank on the edge of town. Avery's eyes lit up.

Ethan noted the delight on her face. "This is the outdoor amphitheatre, rarely used these days. But was once a focal point of the town. We just need to walk down to the bottom of the steps."

She glanced down to the bottom, where the stage centred in the circular stone theatre. Elevated stone benches circled the entire stage. In the centre was a candlelit table set up for two. As they reached the bottom, the stage lit up. String lights formed the illusion of curtains sectioning off their table. Two extra-large lily vases stood elegantly on either side of the stage, filled with pure white lilies.

Rendered speechless, Avery gasped. "Wow, Ethan, this is incredible. I can't believe you did this for me again."

Ethan led her to the centre stage, and they sat down at the beautifully dressed table. Two waiters emerged from the side entrance with a heated trolly and placing a meal in front of them. The waiter corked a bottle of wine and offered a sample for Ethan to taste. He nodded. "Perfect. Thank you." The waiter poured to glasses and then left.

"I hope you don't mind. I ordered salmon for us both. I thought it would be light and fresh. Perfect for a summer night. I made sure to order wild salmon."

"What's the difference? I thought all salmon was fresh."

Ethan studied Avery for a moment. Her innocent curious eyes arrested him. "It depends on what your idea of fresh is. Over recent years a new threat has emerged: floating feedlots on the ocean called open-net salmon farms. The farmed salmon are bred to grow quickly in cages that are so crammed they are rife with parasites and disease. The fish are fed pellets of fishmeal, vegetables, and animal by-products. They are doused regularly with pesticides and antibiotics, too. And I for one, do not want to consume that. I am extremely cautious about what I put into my body.

"I had no idea. I should pay more attention to food labels. Did you use the same catering company?"

"Of course. We only have two weeks, so I want them to be memorable. That way you won't forget me while you are gone," he winked.

"Oh, I think that is very unlikely at this point." Avery paused and searched Ethan's face. His eyes gleamed.

She continued. "Tell me more about you, Ethan. What do you do for a living?"

"Well, I own my own company. Digital security and all things IT. Companies hire us to remove viruses from their network, install firewalls and extra digital protection to ensure their systems are as safe as possible from hackers and the competition. It's an immense business. The biggest threat to big business these days is digital theft, hacking and exposing companies' secrets. Our job is to prevent that from happening and that is why they hire us."

Ethan paused, took a sip of wine, and continued.

"It has taken five years to reach the comfortable position we are in now. It was tough to begin with. Acquiring clients and building your brand is extremely difficult in the beginning. I persevered, and here we are."

Avery was more than impressed. Ethan continually surprised her, and she loved everything about him.

"And your family, you mentioned you had a brother last night. But what about parents?"

Ethan fell silent and turned away briefly. A shadow of sadness crossed his face.

"Ethan, I'm sorry. You don't have to talk about them."

He turned around to face her. "It's fine, really. Both my parents passed away four years ago. It was a hit-and-run accident. They died on impact. Felt nothing, they informed us. My brother took it extremely hard. After the funeral, he went travelling around the world for a year. Then finally settled in Australia. Other than that, there is not much more to tell."

Avery swiftly changed the subject. "So, who were the guys you were with the night we met you at Antonio's restaurant?"

"They were regular clients that I was entertaining after renewing their contract with us."

"So, you don't know them on a personal level?"

"Not particularly. I take them out to dinner occasionally and that's it. Our connection does not extend beyond business."

"I was curious because of Dillon. He is going on a date with Willow on Wednesday."

Ethan raised a brow. "I get it. You want to know if he is a decent guy and your friend is in good hands, right?"

"That about sums it up!"

"Well, from what I know of Dillon, he is a decent guy. He is single. I think Willow is in safe hands."

"Well, that's a relief. You have surpassed yourself this evening. Thank you again for going to so much effort for me. I appreciate it."

"It's my immense pleasure. So, what do you do with your free time?"

Avery thought about his question before answering. "Well, I like hiking and photography. So, I often combine both passions. When I have a spare weekend, I head over to Woodberry Creek. Hike through the forest, eat lunch by the riverside and take photos along the way. It is one of my favourite places to go. Willow joins me sometimes and we will spend most of the day there."

"Maybe you could take me some time," suggested Ethan.

"I would love that."

They talked for hours. Ethan glanced at the time on his phone. "It's getting late, though. I don't know where the time went! It's gone midnight already. I have an early start tomorrow. A new client to impress. So, we better get going."

Avery climbed to her feet. "Of course. I understand."

They slowly made their way up the steps and left the amphitheatre behind. Ethan paused at the car, and without warning, pulled Avery close to him, took her face in his hands, and placed his warm lips on hers. Avery's breathing rapidly increased as Ethan held her close and ran his fingers passionately through her hair. He gently pulled away. "I have been wanting to do that all evening!"

Avery's heart pounded. Her eyes gleamed, barely catching her breath before hopping into the car. Ethan paused, turned to Avery, and searched her face. "You are the best thing to happen to me in a long time."

Avery brushed a stray hair from her face and dipped her eyes, unsure how to respond. She offered a warm smile. Ethan gave her a wink and started the car.

Avery couldn't believe her luck. Happiness coursed through her like a steam train, making her feel giddy.

Ethan drove the short distance to Avery's house and parked on the side of the road. Avery climbed out, turned to Ethan, and paused.

"Tuesday, night at eight o'clock!" he blurted.

Avery's brows drew together. "Tuesday. Mmm, I will have to check my diary," she teased.

"Eight o'clock! Until then, Avery Masters."

Ethan pulled away, and Avery could barely take her eyes off the road until he disappeared from her sight. "Wow!" she said aloud.

CHAPTER EIGHT

*a*very's eyes flickered open. She raised her hand to block out the light pouring through a gap in the curtains. Her thoughts flashed to the night before as she stretched her arms, sporting a wide smile. Ethan dominated her mind. She leapt out of bed and made her way downstairs to make a coffee. Everything felt different this morning. She felt different: she was happy. She poured a coffee and sat down. *I need music this morning* "Alexa, play the best of noughties R&B."

Music echoed around the kitchen. Avery sipped her coffee while reliving her kiss with Ethan. She closed her eyes and imagined his lips pressing against hers. His large masculine hands wrapped around her made Avery feel safe and she liked that feeling. Something to which she was not accustomed.

Her mobile phone vibrating startled her. Willow's number flashed on the screen.

"Hey!"

"Never mind, 'hey.' How did it go last night?"

"It was incredible. He made every effort to impress again. You remember the old amphitheatre on the edge of town?"

"Yes, it has not been used for years!"

"Well, he hired Dream Dates again. This time, it was there. On the centre stage, all lit up with dinner and waiters, too."

"Ethan's smitten for sure. That is amazing. I am happy for you. You deserve this, Avery."

"Thanks. I like him, Willow. I like him a lot."

"I gathered that! Look, I know I encouraged this, but just be sure to take it at your pace, okay?"

"I will. Don't worry. Ethan is the perfect gentleman. To be honest, I can't believe a man like him is even single. Ethan could have any woman he chooses. I have no idea what he sees in me, to be honest."

Willow sighed down the phone. "You can stop that talk right now. Your problem is you don't see your worth. Yes, Ethan is a catch for sure, however, he is the lucky one. Whatever happened to you in your past has stripped you of all your confidence and self-worth. I know you don't like talking about your past and that is fine. But just know that you are worthy of wonderful things. So, no more putting yourself down and that's an order." Willow took a breath.

"Thanks, Willow. You always know the right thing to say. And that is why you are my best friend."

"That's what I'm here for! Now, are we still on for tomorrow night?"

"I'm so sorry. I completely forgot about that and committed to a third date with Ethan."

A long pause ensued.

"Willow, you there?"

"Yes, I'm here. Look, don't worry. We can catch up anytime. I get it. You are in the throes of a new relationship. I recall how heady that can be. It can intoxicate you."

"You sure?" pressed Avery.

"I'm sure. Look, I must dash. I handed in my notice yesterday. I want to leave with good references. Just keep Thursday night free. It's my last day at the company and we are going for drinks after work. I am using some holiday I had left to leave the company early. So, I only have to work a four-day notice. I will need to bring you up to speed about my upcoming date on Wednesday with Dillon too. Oh, next week it's my birthday, remember, and I want to dine at home with you, Lucy, Jackson, and Ruby. Bring Ethan with you. It would be nice to meet him."

"I will be there, and I'll mention it to Ethan. I cannot wait for you all to meet him."

"Same here. Now I really must go. Don't forget Thursday," finished Willow.

"I promise I'll be there. Exciting times are ahead. This will be the making of you, Willow. I can feel it. I'm happy for you. Good luck with your date on Wednesday, not that you need it! See you Thursday." Avery ended the call and placed her phone on the countertop. Her doorbell echoed through the house. She rushed to the front door and opened it. An older man in a hurry greeted her.

"A delivery for Miss Masters."

Avery took the large, elongated box from the courier, thanked him, and shut the door.

She made her way to the kitchen and reached for a pair of scissors from the drawer and cut along the top of the box. She peeked inside and gasped!

Oh, my God! She eased the wrapped bouquet from the box. Her eyes trailed the beautiful arrangement and her mouth dropped open. The large summer arrangement of lilies and bright green stems blew her away. She pulled the small card attached to one stem and read it.

> *I can't stop thinking about you.*
> *Looking forward to Tuesday.*
>
> *Ethan xxx*

Avery re-read the card, focusing on three kisses at the end of the message, and then placed it in a drawer. Happiness surged through her entire body, unlike anything she'd experienced before. Reaching for her phone, she snapped several photos and then sent them to Willow, captioned, *look what just arrived!*

An immediate response pinged back. *Ethan is falling for you fast!*

Avery messaged Ethan:

Thank you so much for the flowers. See you
soon x

Tuesday night came around fast. Avery saw Ethan pull up outside, reached for her keys and headed out the door. Ethan greeted her with a huge smile.

"You look stunning," he said, while his eyes trailed over her pale blue summer tea dress.

"Thank you," replied Avery while climbing into the car.

"Now, this evening I have something much simpler planned. I am cooking dinner for you at my place."

"Really?"

"Yep. The man cooks!" he laughed.

"Now this I have to bear witness to!"

Ethan kissed her on the side of the cheek and drove off towards his house on the edge of Cotswood Town. It didn't take long before he pulled into his driveway. He parked up, and they climbed out. Avery glanced over the four-bed detached house in awe.

"This is stunning," she commented.

"I like it. It suits my needs for now."

"A house like this would suit my needs forever," gushed Avery.

Ethan unlocked the door and stepped aside, allowing Avery to walk in first. "Go on through to the kitchen."

Avery found her way down a wide hallway to the kitchen. She looked around in awe. Her eyes rested on the lantern roof centred over the marble island. She smiled when she saw the stars and moon. "This is stunning!"

Ethan stepped up behind her, slipped his hands around her

waist and spun her around to face him. "No, you're stunning, Avery Masters."

He cupped her face in his hands and kissed her. She responded eagerly. Ethan glided his hand along her back and Avery froze.

"What's the matter?"

Avery turned away from him. "Before we take this any further, I need to share something with you."

She took a long pause, not knowing how to tell him. Ethan fixed a concerned gaze on her.

He inched closer and raised a hand to her cheek and stroked it. "Nothing you tell me could change my mind about you," he reassured her.

Avery drew a long, deep breath. "Something happened to me when I was a child, well, more of a young teenager. I was beaten badly, and it left some harsh scars on my back. I felt you should know before we went any further."

Avery didn't offer any further explanation. She turned away from Ethan again, swiping a tear from her cheek.

Ethan slipped his hands around her waist and pulled her to him. "Nothing you can tell me will change my mind about you, I promise you."

She turned around and kissed him. Ethan took her hand and led her upstairs to his bedroom. He ran his fingers through her silky hair. "If this is not okay, just say the word and we can go back downstairs."

"This is okay," she smiled nervously.

Ethan turned her around and slowly unzipped her tea dress, allowing it to fall to the floor. He paused momentarily, then traced her scars with his fingers, kissing each one before spinning her around, picking her up and placing her down on the bed gently. He slipped off his clothes and slipped on top of her. Avery wrapped her hands around his back as he entered her slowly. Avery gasped, her head fell back, and they both lost themselves in the moment. Climaxing together, in perfect sync with one another. Ethan slipped off her and lay on his side, stroking her hair. Then he preceded to kiss every inch of her body. He did not mention her scars again. He knew she had offered all that she was going to about them.

Sometime later, Ethan leapt off the bed. "Now, about me cooking us dinner!"

Avery fell about laughing as Ethan headed for a quick shower. Once he finished, Avery followed suit and made use of his luxurious wet room while Ethan headed downstairs to prepare dinner.

CHAPTER NINE

*W*illow attempted calling Avery, to no avail. Once again, she left a long message. Furious, she turned to her sister. "I have barely seen her this week. We were supposed to meet up Thursday at the Renaissance Bar in town to celebrate my last day at work and she didn't show. Avery knew full well I needed her support. She has returned none of my messages. There's no excuse for this, Lucy."

"That doesn't sound like Avery. I'm guessing she has gotten all caught up in the romance of it all. You know what new love feels like. It consumes you in the beginning. Well, just imagine how it feels for Avery. She has never been in love, let alone had a meaningful relationship. It's fair to say Ethan has swept her off her feet."

Willow huffed. "Literally!" she retorted.

Lucy raised her brow. "Stop stressing. Avery will come back down to earth before long."

Willow's phone vibrated in her pocket. She retrieved it, gasped, and glanced at Lucy in shock. "It's Avery!"

She swiped to answer. "Where the hell have you been?" demanded Willow.

"I'm so sorry. Ethan whisked me away on our third date for a few days. We spent the first night at his house and then we drove out to a beautiful lakeside lodge at Wicker's Forest. I lost my phone and couldn't make calls."

"You could have used Ethan's phone to call me, or did you forget about meeting me on Thursday?"

"Oh, no...I'm so sorry. It escaped my mind. There is no excuse, Willow. Again, I'm sorry. I will make it up to you. I thought about using Ethan's phone to call you, but I didn't know your number. Ridiculous as it sounds, I never have to physically type your number. It's stored in my contacts. I just tap your name."

"I get that. I don't know anyone's number off by heart either. I could not recite yours if I needed to."

"Don't worry about it. I was just worried about you. It was so unlike you, that's all."

"I understand. Ethan has consumed me, Willow. He wants to make the most of our time together before I leave for work in a few days. We have spent most days together. I think he is the one!"

"Seriously?"

"Yes, I just know it."

Willow chimed in. "But it's only been eight days! Things are moving fast. Well, all that matters is that you're happy. So did you find your phone in the end?"

"Weirdly, Ethan found it on the floor under the back seat of the car this morning. I don't know how it got there. Anyway, you were the first person I called. Are you free later?"

"Yes, I can be," confirmed Willow.

"Then pop over to my house and we can catch up properly. I want to hear how your last day at work went and your date with Dillon."

"I can be at yours around two-ish, does that work?"

"Perfect. I will prepare a late lunch for us. See you later," finished Avery.

Willow slipped her phone into her pocket and turned to her

sister. "This is so unlike Avery. I have never known her like this. She's like a different person altogether."

Lucy's brow furrowed. "It all sounds intense. What happened to her phone?"

Willow shook her head, annoyed. "Apparently, she lost it. Ethan found it under the back seat of his car this morning while cleaning it. It's not that I don't believe her, but it just doesn't sit right with me. None of it does. Ethan is moving too fast, and you know how delicate and vulnerable Avery is."

Lucy ambled over to Willow and placed her hand on her arm. "I will tell you what I think. Avery has fallen in love even if she doesn't realise it yet. This is all knew to her. Love makes people dizzy and forgetful. Don't worry. Avery is an intelligent woman. I am sure she knows what she is doing."

Willow nodded in agreement. "I'm sure you're right."

"I know I am right. You're overthinking it. And remember, you have never seen her like this before because you have never seen Avery in love before. It changes people."

"You're right, as always. Anyway, has Jackson been in touch. I have not heard from him?"

Lucy glanced out of the window and smiled. "Funny you should mention Jackson. Our brother is closer than you think!"

The front door swung open, and Jackson entered, pushing Ruby in front of him.

Willow darted to him. "Oh my God, why didn't you tell me you were coming today? You weren't due until tomorrow."

Jackson lifted Ruby out of the pushchair, and before he could say anything, Lucy swiped her from his arms. "Aunty Lucy needs some Ruby time. I will leave you two to catch up."

Willow noticed the tired look on Jackson's face. He appeared thinner, too.

"Hey, why don't I make some coffee?" suggested Willow.

"Sounds great. I need one." Jackson took off his jacket and hung it over the chair.

Willow pottered in the kitchen preparing their coffee while Jackson pulled up a stool at the kitchen island. "How have you been?" he asked.

Willow placed two cups of coffee on the centre island. "Never mind me for now. I want to know how you are coping?"

Jackson lowered his eyes, reached for his coffee, and took a sip. "Truth is, Willow, it's tough being a single dad. There, I've said it. I am knackered all the time. I have been at this single father thing for over a year now and it hasn't gotten any easier. But I wouldn't have it any other way. Ruby is my life, and she comes first, no matter what."

"Well, just remember you have two eager babysitters here whenever you need a rest."

Jackson's lips curled. "I know, and I will call on both of you soon. I have an out-of-town business trip for a few days."

"Great, I would love to spend more time with Ruby, and I know Lucy doesn't need asking twice. Just say when and it's done."

"Thanks, Sis. I appreciate it."

Willow pondered her next question. She knew it was a sensitive area. "How are you dealing with your grief?"

Jackson stood and went to the window, keeping his back to Willow.

"Ruby helps with that a great deal. It's the evenings that are the hardest. Going to bed alone. I miss sharing my day with her. I thought Janine and I would be together until old age. Her death was so premature. I will never forgive that drunk driver for what he did to my family. I try hard to focus on Ruby. I cannot sink into despair. As you know, I almost did. If it were not for you, Lucy, and Avery, I don't know what I would have done. But here we are surviving," Jackson trailed off in thought.

Willow placed her hand over his. "This is your home too, and don't you forget it. If ever you need to take some time out, Lucy and I would be happy to have Ruby for a while. You don't have to do this alone."

"Thanks. And I know you have my back, you both do. Now tell me, how's Avery doing? Lucy tells me she has finally got herself a boyfriend. I must admit, I never thought I'd see the day, due to how closed off she is. She barely goes out!"

"Yep, and she is smitten. Honestly, I have never seen her like this. I hardly recognise her these days."

"Did she ever fully confide her childhood to you?"

"Not really. Avery is closed off about that. She revealed snippets here and there over the years, but nothing more than that. I think it is too harrowing for her to relive. I do know that her mother abused her and locked her up in her room many times. But that's all I know. Her home life was not good. I never pushed her to tell me more than she was willing to share. The day will come when she will be ready."

"It's been almost seven years, Willow. I doubt she will share more than she has after all this time. It makes sense why she is so private and untrusting of people, though. I'm just glad she has you."

"Yeh, me too. By the way, you know that you and Lucy are cooking my birthday dinner tomorrow night?"

"Lucy informed me this morning. Happy to do it, Sis. Do you think Avery will turn up?"

Willow rolled her eyes. "She'd better. She's my best friend and must be there. I told her she could bring Ethan."

Jackson raised a curious brow. "I can't wait to meet the man who has whisked Avery off her feet." He trailed off in thought, falling silent, which did not go unnoticed by Willow.

"I met him briefly that night at Antonio's" she said. "He seemed like the mysterious type. Exceptionally handsome, too."

Jackson chimed in. "Of course, he is. Avery is stunning, so I'm not surprised."

Avery noticed Jackson's shift in mood at the mention of Avery dating.

"You okay, Jackson?"

"Yes, why wouldn't I be?"

"Okay, if you're sure."

Before Jackson could respond, Lucy bounded into the kitchen with Ruby, changing the mood. Jackson smiled widely as his daughter tottered around to Willow, who knelt on the floor with her arms outstretched. "Come here, you little beauty." She swept her up in her arms and hugged her. "I've missed you."

"I was thinking we could go out for lunch today. What do you all think?"

"Mmm, count me in. The idea of having food cooked for me these days is a luxury!" chimed Jackson.

"I'm in, but I can only have a drink. Avery is cooking lunch for me today. I'm due at her house around two-ish," informed Willow.

Willow bounced Ruby on her lap. "And what about you, Miss Ruby Forbes?" Ruby giggled and climbed off Willow. She tottered around the kitchen island to her dad.

"Come here, Princess," he said, scooping her up in his arms.

"You're so good with Ruby. She is lucky to have you as her father."

Jackson shook his head. "No. I'm the lucky one. Without Ruby, I would have fallen apart for sure. She has held me together."

Lucy held her arms outstretched. "I feel a family hug coming on!" Jackson and Willow shook their heads mockingly and joined Lucy in a group hug." Ruby wriggled free to the floor,

"Okay. Shall we leave in fifteen minutes? That's enough time to sort yourself out," suggested Lucy.

Nodding their heads in unison, Jackson and Willow agreed.

CHAPTER TEN

Ethan straightened his jacket as he approached Avery's door. He knocked and stood back patiently.

Upon opening the door, Avery swooped in for a hug. "Hey, I wasn't expecting to see you today. Come in."

Ethan followed behind her through to the kitchen.

"Take a seat. I was just making some fresh coffee. Would you like one?"

"I'd love one, thanks."

Ethan's eyes followed Avery around the kitchen. Her pale blue cotton maxi dress brushed against the wooden floor as she moved. His eyes rested on her wavy hair falling down her back and he drew in a deep breath.

Sensing his eyes on her, Avery spun around. "What is it?"

"Nothing. I was just watching you."

"Mmm, I see!"

Avery walked over to him and planted a kiss on his lips. He wrapped his hands around her waist, pulling her closer. "I think I'm in trouble!"

"Trouble?"

"Oh yes, big trouble."

"And why is that?"

"You have stolen my heart and I don't know what to do about that!"

Avery inched closer, their noses almost touching. "Why do anything at all?"

"You're right. I shall leave my heart in your hands and trust it will be safe."

"It's safe." Avery kissed him once more and then pulled away to pour their coffee. "Willow is dropping by shortly."

"Oh, right? Yes, of course, you made plans. It was just an impromptu visit. I won't stay long."

"Look, why don't you stay?" suggested Avery.

"I don't want to intrude on your girl time."

"Willow won't mind at all. It's just lunch. I insist. By the way, Willow's having a birthday dinner at home tomorrow evening, and you are invited too. It's an intimate dinner with her closest friends."

"Well then, how can I refuse? I would love to go."

Smiling from ear to ear, Avery balanced on her toes and kissed him on the lips.

"You can help me prepare lunch for us. Why don't you prep the salad while I pop the peppers under the grill?" she said, while floating around the kitchen like a breath of fresh air.

Ethan navigated around Avery in the kitchen, stealing the occasional kiss while he prepped and tossed the salad. Background music played and the smell of roasting peppers brought a smile to Ethan's face. Avery laid the table and pulled the char-grilled red peppers from under the grill. Ethan retrieved the dips from the fridge and poured the wine. Knocking on the door raised their attention. "That must be Willow. She is uncharacteristically punctual today!" she opened the door and teased, "I think I am seeing things."

"Whatever do you mean?" replied Willow breezing past her into the house.

"You are on time. You're never early!"

"Yes, I can see how that would be confusing," she joked.

Willow's smile disappeared from her face when she caught sight of Ethan laying out cutlery on the kitchen table.

"Willow, it's great to meet you properly. I have heard wonderful things about you."

Willow forced a smile. "Hi, Ethan. I wasn't aware you were joining us for lunch."

Ethan noted the uncomfortable shift between them and attempted to ease the situation. "I'm sorry. It's my fault. I dropped by on the off-chance Avery was in. Completely ignoring she might have made plans. I did offer to leave, but Avery insisted I stay."

Willow's brows snapped together. "Of course, she did."

Avery entered the kitchen and sensed an atmosphere. "Ethan stopped by, and I thought he could join us for lunch. I hope you don't mind, and I have been eager for you to meet him."

Willow shook her head. "Of course not. Now, what are we eating?" she asked, lightening the mood.

"My cheese-topped roasted pepper salad speciality. I know how much you love it."

"Sounds lovely."

Willow turned to Ethan. "Did Avery mention my birthday dinner tomorrow?"

"Yes, thank you for inviting me along. I look forward to it," he confirmed, navigating around Avery.

Willow removed her jacket, hung it over her chair and sat at the table, observing the interaction between Ethan and Avery as they busied in the kitchen. After a few minutes, Ethan sensed Willow's eyes on him. He spun around and cast an icy glare her way.

Ethan continued to cast the occasional frosty glare at Willow, and it unnerved her. Ethan spoke first when they sat at the table.

"Avery tells me you are starting your own business?"

Willow turned to Avery, surprised, and then back to Ethan. "Yes, I am."

Avery observed Willow's tone with Ethan and cast a questionable glance her way.

"And I believe you are into web design?" Ethan continued.

"I am yes, amongst other things."

Avery searched Willow's face. "So, how did your date with Dillon go?" she chimed in.

Willow cast a harsh glance towards Avery. "It went fine. But that's girl talk. I will tell you about it when we are alone."

"I'm sorry. I wasn't thinking. Of course, you don't want to discuss it with Ethan here."

Once again, Avery shifted the conversation. "So, what's new?"

Willow softened. "Jackson arrived a day early. He surprised me this morning. You should see Ruby now. She has grown so much and talking more, too."

"How is Jackson doing?"

"He's coping as best as he can. Doing better than he was. He looks tired, though. But that will be remedied in a few days with Lucy and me. He can catch up on some much-needed sleep and recharge."

"Please tell Jackson I asked after him. Hug him for me and Ruby, too."

"I will. He asked after you as well. Anyway, you will see him tomorrow. He can't wait to catch up with you. Willow's eyes shifted to Ethan. She noted the disapproving look on his face at the mention of Jackson and found his silent response unnerving.

Ethan chimed in. "And who's Jackson?"

Avery jumped in to answer before Willow had a chance. "Jackson is Willow's brother. And a friend of mine through Willow. Sadly, he lost his wife in an accident just over a year ago and is now bringing up their daughter alone."

"I'm sorry to hear that, Willow. It must be tough for him."

Willow nodded at Ethan and turned to Avery. "It's been a while since we have all been together."

"It has been way too long," agreed Avery.

She pointed to the apple pie. "Well, who's up for dessert?"

Willow stood up. "I can't, sorry. I have a Zoom call this afternoon and I need to get home to prepare." She caught Ethan's eyes boring through her and turned away.

"I will call you tomorrow. Enjoy your dessert. I can let myself out." She reached for her jacket off the back of the chair and left.

Avery looked bewildered by Willow's swift departure. "I'm sorry. I don't know what's gotten into Willow. I have never seen her act that way before. She has a lot on. She must be anxious about her new business and her brother is visiting for a few days with her niece. Her business is a huge undertaking and all new to her," Avery explained.

"No need to apologise. I understand. It's difficult setting up on your own. I know all too well the obstacles new business owners face."

CHAPTER ELEVEN

*W*illow dashed down the stairs to open the door. Her eyes widened. "A parcel for Willow Forbes."

Willow smiled at the courier. "Yes, that's me."

"Sign here, please."

Willow signed the digital box and closed the door. "Wow!" She glanced over the beautiful summer bouquet arrangement sitting perfectly in a custom luxury gift bag that did not disappoint. Foliage complimented the grandeur encased with golden orbits, gleaming in the sunlight beaming through the kitchen window.

Lucy gasped as she entered. "Wow! they are beautiful. Who are they from?"

Willow reached for the card lodged securely in the bouquet and read it: "Aww, they are from Avery and Ethan. Avery never disappoints."

"Speaking of Avery, is Ethan coming tonight?"

Willow nodded. "I believe so. Avery confirmed he was."

"Well then. We finally get to see what all the fuss is about!"

Willow did not comment, and her silence was not lost on Lucy. "What's up?"

"Oh, it's nothing. I'm just being silly and paranoid."

Lucy's brows fused curiously. "Well, let me be the judge of that."

"No, really, it's nothing. Now, what are you and Jackson cooking tonight? You've both been very cagy about it."

"Ah, that would be telling. That's why it's called a surprise dinner!"

Jackson wandered into the kitchen, holding Ruby on his hip. "Morning. Nice flowers!"

Willow piped up. "They are from Willow and Ethan."

Jackson stole a stem from the enormous bouquet and handed it to Ruby.

She gushed and climbed down his leg, taking the flower, and sniffing it.

Jackson headed over to Willow and kissed her cheek. "Happy Birthday, Sis."

"Thank you. Now, I am going into town for a couple of hours to buy a new dress for myself and get my hair done. I shall see you guys later."

Once Willow left, Jackson and Lucy sprang into action, preparing for Willow's birthday dinner. They hung balloons and a large banner in the dining room. Dressed the table with a table runner, placemats and napkins finished with a floral centre piece. Once finished, they both stood back and admired their handy work.

"I think Willow will love it," admired Jackson.

"Yep. She better!" chimed Lucy, straightening the runner.

Jackson caught Ruby as she ran past them and headed straight for the table. "Oh no, you don't." He scooped her up and spun her around.

"She is growing fast."

"Tell me about it. She's into everything right now. Since she started walking, she's been like lightning around the house! The girl is fast."

Lucy held her arms out. "Pass her over. I need Ruby time."

Jackson handed Ruby over to Lucy. Thanks, I could do with five minutes. I have a couple of calls to make."

Lucy nodded. "You make your calls. I got this." Lucy hitched Ruby on her hip and headed to the kitchen.

* * *

Seven pm was approaching and Avery put the final changes to her makeup.

Ethan walked up behind her and kissed her neck. He noted the low neckline. "You look stunning. I hope you don't mind me saying, I think the blue dress suited you more."

Avery swivelled around in her chair, stood up and glanced at herself in the mirror. "Really, you think so?"

"Both dresses are stunning, I just think the blue highlights your eyes. Your choice, though. Beautiful either way."

"Maybe you're right. Pass me the blue dress and I'll make a quick change."

Ethan turned around and smirked while picking up the dress. "Here you go."

"Thanks." Avery made a quick change and looked in the mirror. "You're right. The blue does look better."

Ethan ambled up behind her, "Like I said, stunning!"

She beamed. "You don't look so bad yourself."

"Are you ready?"

"I'm ready. I will meet you downstairs."

Avery ran her fingers through her hair and slipped on her shoes before heading downstairs. Ethan reached for his car keys off the coffee table, and they left.

* * *

Jackson turned off the oven and gathered the plates while Lucy corked the wine.

"Almost ready. Avery and Ethan should be here soon."

Willow breezed into the dining room and gasped. "This is amazing. Thank you. So, this is why I wasn't allowed in here all day!"

Lucy looped Willow's arm. "We wanted it to be special for you."

Willow glanced from Lucy and then to Jackson. "I am so lucky to have you guys. It's a shame Mum and Dad couldn't be here."

"We will see them soon enough," commented Jackson.

"Now, let's have our first toast of the night," insisted Jackson, waving a bottle of wine in the air.

He poured three glasses of wine and held up his glass. "To Willow. Our craziest sibling!" he toasted.

Lucy nodded. "To Willow, the crazy one," she laughed.

"Okay, enough with the crazy jokes."

They turned when the doorbell rang. "That must be Avery and Ethan," beamed Willow, heading straight for the door.

Lucy shot a glance at Jackson, who raised a curious brow.

Willow returned swiftly, followed by Avery and Ethan. Willow made the introductions. "Hey guys, this is Ethan."

Jackson wasted no time in heading straight over to Ethan with an extended hand. "Great to meet you, Ethan. I'm Jackson."

"Likewise," said Ethan, shaking Jackson's hand firmly.

"And I'm Lucy."

"Lovely to meet you, Lucy." Ethan reluctantly stepped back, sizing Jackson up as Avery made her way over and hugged him. "It's so good to see you. It's been way too long."

As he let Avery go, Jackson noticed a strange look flash across Ethan's face. *Jealousy!* Apparently, Lucy caught it and flashed her eyes to Willow.

Willow raised her brows in a silent acknowledgement. Ethan was quick to fix a smile on his face as he observed the interaction between Avery and Jackson. Jackson's obvious good looks and height did not go unnoticed by Ethan. Who stood an inch taller than him.

* * *

Lucy looped Ethan's arm and guided him out of the living room. "Come on, I will show you through to the dining room." Hesitantly, Ethan followed, while casting a glance Jackson's way as he left the room.

"So, you've certainly made an impression on Avery," Lucy blurted.

"Avery is special," commented Ethan.

"Yep. She sure is. She is also fragile and needs treating with care."

Ethan noted Lucy's concern. "Avery is in excellent hands."

"That's what I like to hear. Now, this is your seat," pointed Lucy.

Ethan pulled out a chair and sat down. Avery and Jackson entered, and Lucy was quick to guide them to their seats. "Avery, you are seated over there opposite Ethan, and Jackson, you are beside Avery."

Ethan's face dimmed. He cast a glance at Jackson and held his gaze. Jackson turned away, unfazed, and continued to chat with Avery.

Ethan piped up. "So, Jackson, Avery tells me you're a single dad. Can't be easy."

Silence gripped the room. Then Ruby came tottering in with Willow. Jackson beamed and held out his arms as Ruby ran into them. He turned back to Ethan. "Yes. I don't know how much Avery told you, but I lost my wife just over a year ago."

Ethan's face softened. "I'm sorry to hear that." His eyes shifted to Ruby. "She is beautiful. You must be so proud of her."

"I am. Ruby has kept me going."

Willow jumped in and swiftly changed the subject. "Let's have a toast!" she held up her glass. Everyone else reached for their glasses and they held them up. "To good friends and family."

They toasted in unison. Ethan's eyes shifted back to Jackson. Lucy caught the moment and kicked Willow's foot under the table.

Willow observed the look of disdain etched all over Ethan's face. Annoyed, she piped up. "Jackson you must tell Avery about your promotion."

"Yes, tell me," Avery pressed.

"They made me partner in the firm."

"No way! That's amazing." Avery leapt from her chair and over to Jackson, enveloping him in a tight hug. "Congratulations. You deserve this. I am so happy for you."

"Thanks, Avery."

Ethan's face flushed with disapproval at their embrace. His eyes followed Avery back to her chair. He glared at her for the longest time.

"Is everything okay, Ethan?" Lucy asked.

Ethan snapped back to the present moment and smiled. "Yes, I think the wine has gone to my head. I have barely eaten today."

Puzzled by his comment, Avery piped up. "But you had a huge lunch?"

Ethan fixed his eyes on Avery and glared at her momentarily.

"Yes, but I skipped breakfast. Lunch was hours ago."

Avery nodded in agreement. "Of course. Speaking of which, I'm hungry, too."

Lucy and Jackson leapt up from their seats and scurried off into the kitchen. Willow took Ruby to the toilet, leaving Avery and Ethan alone.

Avery noticed the change in Ethan's mood. "What's wrong?"

"I thought that was obvious,"

"No. It's not. So why don't you enlighten me?"

"You are embarrassing me, Avery. You were all over Jackson. Friend or not, it's just not appropriate."

Avery's jaw dropped. Before she could respond, Lucy and Jackson entered the room with plates in hand.

"Here you go, Avery." Lucy carefully placed the dinner plate down on the table. Jackson walked over to Ethan and repeated Lucy's action. "Enjoy."

"This looks amazing. Thank you," said Ethan.

"Lucy did most of the cooking. I was simply her sous-chef!"

Willow burst through the door with Ruby and sat her in the highchair beside her. "Here you go, Sis. Your favourite dish of all time," said Lucy. "Jackson and I tried our best to replicate mum's special for you."

"Oh, you guys! It looks amazing. Mum's fish plait with roasted garlic, sweet potatoes and pan-fried asparagus with chestnut mushrooms. It's been too long since I've had this."

Jackson chimed in. "Lucy has been on the phone to mum for most of the afternoon to make sure she got it right."

"Yeh, and I still can't promise it will taste anything like mum's recipe!"

They all started eating and Willow noticed the change in Avery's mood. She was eating slowly and picking at her food. "Avery, everything okay?"

"Yes, it's lovely."

She turned to Lucy. "You did an amazing job."

Awkward moments of silence filled the rest of the evening. Ethan's mood switched often, which did not go unnoticed.

After dessert, Ethan looked at Avery, indicating for them to leave. "It's been a lovely evening. Thanks for inviting me. I have an early start tomorrow, so I better be going." He gave Avery a nod. "You ready?"

She stood up. "Thanks for dinner. You guys did a fabulous job." She bent down and hugged Ruby. "See you soon, Princess."

Then she extended her arms and hugged Willow. "Happy birthday, bestie!"

Avery turned to Jackson, and then back to Ethan deciding against hugging him. "Bye Jackson, see you soon."

Jackson offered a knowing smile. "Bye Avery. Take care. See you soon."

Avery and Ethan left the house, leaving the rest of them flabbergasted.

"Well?" blurted Lucy.

Jackson shook his head. "I don't like him. There is something not quite right about him."

Willow nodded. "I feel the same. I realised Ethan does not approve of your friendship with Avery. It was written all over his face. He could barely hide it. That does not bode well for Avery."

Lucy interrupted. "I agree. However, we barely know Ethan. We must give him the benefit of the doubt. I can't say I'm over-enamoured with him either. However, he can't be that bad if he gained Avery's trust. She has clearly fallen for him."

Jackson walked over to Ruby, lifted her out of the highchair, and wiped her face. "I still don't like him. Trust me, there is something off with that guy. I'm going to put Ruby to bed."

"Did you notice how Avery didn't hug Jackson before she left? She always hugs him!"

Lucy nodded. "I caught that too. After we left them a lone for a few minutes, Avery's mood changed dramatically. I reckon he had words with her. It was clear to me he does not approve of Jackson and Avery's friendship. However, it does not mean he is a bad guy. Time will tell."

Willow shook her head in disagreement. "Mmm, I beg to differ. I'm with Jackson and there is definitely something off with Ethan. Anyway, enough about him. Come here," Willow enveloped Lucy in a tight hug. "You're the best. You did mum proud today. Dinner was incredible."

"You're welcome. I'm just happy you liked it. I'm going to load up the dishwasher and then head off to bed. As it's your birthday, you get a pass!"

"Thanks, sis, I'm shattered too. Thanks for today, it was lovely. Goodnight."

CHAPTER TWELVE

Willow cupped her hands around her coffee mug while Lucy prepared breakfast.

"That smells good. Can I have extra eggs if there's enough? I'm starving this morning."

"There's plenty. Do you want mushrooms with them?"

"No thanks. Just eggs and a slice of toast."

Lucy plated up their breakfast and joined Willow on the kitchen island, pulling out a stool.

"Did Jackson get off okay?" Willow asked.

"Yes. I was going to wake you, but Jackson told me to let you sleep in. He looked refreshed. He needed a break. He's enjoyed his few days with us. I don't know how he does it. I think we need to check in on him more often, though. You know how proud he is. Jackson would never ask for help. Lucky for him, his career pays well. He was telling me how much childcare costs him this morning and I nearly fell off my chair. I don't think I'll be having kids any time soon."

"Same here. You're right though, we need to check in with him more often. Maybe offer to take Ruby off his hands occasionally, so he can get some breathing space," Willow agreed.

"For sure. He said before he left, you should keep an eye on Avery. He doesn't trust Ethan one bit. This whole situation has rattled him."

"Well, we're on the same page. There's not much I can do, though. Avery is smitten. I know you think Jackson and I are overreacting, but I cannot shake this feeling."

Willow checked her WhatsApp messages and huffed. She leapt from her stool and popped her plate into the dishwasher. "Avery has left me on *read*. It takes a second to respond. I haven't heard from her for days. She leaves tomorrow for Africa. Can you believe it?"

Lucy placed the cutlery down. "I cannot pretend to know what is going on with Avery. It's unlike her for sure. And you haven't seen her since she came over for dinner with Ethan a few days ago?"

Willow rolled her eyes. "Nope! She is never available anymore. It's so out of character for her. We went from talking daily for seven years to almost no contact at all. I just don't get it. And Jackson is right to be concerned. There is something off with Ethan. You should have seen the way he looked at me last week over lunch. He views me as a threat, I'm sure."

Lucy shook her head. "I wouldn't go that far. You are overthinking this again. Avery is in love for the first time in her life. It has consumed her. Try to remember the first time you fell in love. I remember all too well. You barely picked up your calls and never returned them. I'm trying to be the voice of reason here."

"I guess you're right. But I still think there is something not right about him. My instincts are never wrong. I am going to drop by Avery's house and catch her before she leaves for Africa."

She finished her coffee and reached for her coat. "Fancy coming with me?"

"Mmm, that'll be a firm no. I am not getting in the middle of whatever is going on between you two. If I were you, I would take a step back and let Avery come to you. When she comes back down to earth, she will realise soon enough that she has been neglectful."

"Thanks for the sisterly advice, but I am heading over to Avery's house right now."

Avery left. Lucy shook her head in disapproval as she watched Avery pull off the driveway.

* * *

An uneasy feeling circled Willow's stomach as she approached Avery's house. She parked in the driveway, climbed out and headed for the door. Willow rang the doorbell and waited. No answer. She rang it three more times, but there was no reply.

"Where the hell is she?" A huge sigh escaped Willow's mouth. *Come on, Avery, answer the door.*

Eventually, she gave up and headed back to her car. She sat there for a few minutes, puzzled. *Surely, she should be home packing,* she mused. She decided to call Avery's boss, to see whether she had left early. She searched her contacts and swiped to call.

"Hello, Jax, it's Willow. I'm sorry to bother you. I am trying to get hold of Avery before she leaves for Africa tomorrow."

"I'm sorry, Willow, you haven't heard. Avery isn't going to Africa. She requested leave. The company owed her a lot of leave and Avery decided the time was right to take it. I signed off on it yesterday."

Speechless, Willow fell silent. "Hello. Willow, you still there?"

"Sorry, Jax. Yes. Thank you." Willow cut the call and swiped Avery's number. To her surprise, Avery answered.

"Hey Willow."

"Avery, where have you been? You have not returned my messages and I was getting worried. It's unlike you."

"I'm sorry. I've been spending a lot of time at Ethan's place. Can you believe I misplaced my phone again? I swear all this romance stuff is turning my brain to mush!"

"But you left my last message on *read?*"

"Oh, I could have sworn I replied. I'm sorry. I have been a terrible friend lately. I will make it up to you."

"I wanted to catch up with you before you left for Africa. As I could not get hold of you, I called Jax."

"Ah, I'm guessing he told you I have taken extended leave?"

"He did, yes. What's going on with you? Your job is your passion. It shocked me when Jax told me."

"To be honest, as the day of my departure grew closer, Ethan and I dreaded the day. Especially Ethan. He suggested I take some leave. After all, the company owed me a fair amount."

"I see. So, it was Ethan's idea?"

"Well, yes, but I liked the thought of extra time with him. We are going on holiday for a couple of weeks."

"Are you sure you know what you are doing, Avery? You have only known him for two weeks."

"Willow, I love you. But I am a grown woman and more than capable of making my own life decisions. I don't understand what's happening here. You encouraged this relationship. I thought you would be happy for me?"

"I am happy for you. I am also concerned, too. What sort of friend would I be if I did not look out for you?"

"I'm sorry I have not been in touch as often as I normally would. That was selfish of me. I promise once I return from Scotland, we will have the biggest catch-up and I will cook dinner. How's that?"

"Sounds lovely. Have a lovely holiday and take lots of pics. I will see you when you get back. Take care."

Willow cut the call and sat back in her car seat, shaking her head. *Something is very wrong with all of this. I need to know more about this Ethan guy. I have a bad feeling.* Willow started the car and headed home.

CHAPTER THIRTEEN

*A*very glanced around the elegant castle Ethan had secured through Airbnb. A stunning Gothic Revival castle built during the Victorian era, impressive, extravagant, and more beautiful than their medieval counterparts.

"This is stunning."

She peeked into the library and the distinctive ornamentation of the walnut furniture and rosewood panelling made her gasp in awe. "Wow, look at the sliding ladders reaching from one end of the library to the other. I have to try them." She ambled over to the ladder and climbed a couple of steps.

"Be careful," Ethan warned.

"I'm fine. I just wanted to experience this in the moment. If you haven't guessed already, I am a bookie and love all things associated with books. Stepping into this library was akin to handing a kid a chocolate box!"

"I am catching on!" commented Ethan as she stepped off the ladder.

Avery stood back and again glanced up at the vaulted ceiling. "We don't see libraries like this too often. They took grandeur to a whole new level. It's a shame we don't design buildings like this anymore. They appreciated books and their worth so much more than people do today. I mean, just look at this room!" Avery paused and inhaled the smell of the books that permeated the library.

"This is my heaven."

Ethan nodded. "I think I get that now! Sadly, everything is about money and speed today. The quicker they can be built and as cost-effective as possible is the goal. There are exceptions to the rule, of course." Ethan laced his fingers through Avery's and led her through the rest of the castle, sneaking kisses along the way. Avery was giddy with happiness and realised this was the first time in her life that she felt truly happy. She was no longer in survival mode–a state of mind that had caused her great anxiety for most of her life.

Ethan continued to advise Avery on the Castle's layout as they breezed from room to room. "The Victorians had a love for gothic revival in the eighteenth century. Over the years, castles like this smaller one became too much for the owners to manage financially. The upkeep and maintenance alone became a burden, so they turned them into hotels, rented them out to corporate businesses or sold them off to private companies who snapped them up and turned them into luxury holiday rentals."

"That's a shame," interrupted Avery.

Ethan continued. "There are four wings. We are staying in the west wing. The further three wings of the castle are hired out to other holiday makers arriving tomorrow, I believe the west wing is our private space."

"Wow! The west wing," Avery chuckled.

Ethan jabbed her arm playfully and continued. "The shared space is the ballroom, library, main dining hall and, of course, the gardens that extend for acres. Each wing comes with its own dedicated chef and butler. We have our own smaller dining room and living area where we shall take our meals. I thought this would be the perfect first holiday for us. It's a small castle compared to most; however, it was the best one for us. I loved the location. There is a large lake beyond the grounds. I thought we could take a walk around it after lunch."

Avery wrapped her hands around Ethan's neck and planted a firm kiss on his lips. "This is like a dream. I have no words." Avery reached for her phone from her pocket.

Ethan was quick to react and swiped it out of her hand. "My only request for our first holiday is no phones. I have turned mine off already."

Avery smiled. "You're right. Let's be in the moment."

Ethan turned off her phone and slipped it into his pocket. They continued to explore the west wing of the castle before changing clothes and heading out onto the landscaped grounds that stretched far and wide. Two gardeners nodded as they passed them. Ethan ignored them while Avery cast a warm smile their way.

"Willow would love this place."

Ethan didn't respond.

"This is the first time I have holidayed without Willow. We have always done everything together."

Ethan raised an eyebrow and chimed in. "Then it was certainly long overdue. There is an entire world out there for us to explore together," he responded, emphasizing *together*.

"So, you have thought that far ahead?"

"Of course, haven't you?" he pressed.

"I've been so caught up in the moment, I haven't thought of anything else."

Ethan stopped them in their tracks and turned to Avery. "When I think about my future, I see you right by my side." He brushed a stray hair from her face and swept her cheek with his hand.

Avery was speechless. She searched his face, and, at that moment, she realised she had fallen in love with him. "I love you," she confessed, surprising herself.

A huge smile raised on Ethan's face. He cupped her face in his hands and placed his lips on hers. "I love you too. You have no idea how happy you've made me. I think we should explore the bedroom!" he winked, lacing his fingers through hers.

They ran back to the castle, laughing along the way. When they reached the grand bedroom, Ethan slipped off his shoes and held out his hand. Avery placed her hand in his and he pulled her onto the bed. He sat up and began undressing her slowly while his eyes were locked on hers. Avery's chest rose and fell with rapid breaths. Ethan slipped off her underwear and then undressed eagerly. His large hands coasted the length of her lithe, toned body and he marvelled at the softness of her skin.

"You're so beautiful," he whispered while circling her belly button with his tongue. Avery's back arched and Ethan slipped his large hands around her. Avery's body gyrated. Ethan gasped with pleasure as he gripped her thighs, encouraging her to move faster. Avery flung her head back as the heat pulsed through her veins. Ethan pressed harder against her groin, going deeper inside of her. She groaned and gyrated rhythmically; her eyes rolled back as the intensity of the moment stepped up to another level. Close to climax, Ethan moaned, sliding his hands up to the centre of her back and pulling her in close.

"I want all of you, Avery Masters. You are mine now."

Avery's back arched once more as her legs stiffened, falling prey to his prowess as they climaxed together. Merging as one in the moment.

* * *

Over the next two weeks, their connection grew strong. Exploring the Scottish countryside by day and making love at night. They spent every minute of every day together. They took their last evening meal out by Loch Lomond. The chef prepared a large picnic and Ethan retrieved a blanket from their room.

"I am going to miss this place," commented Avery.

"Yeh, me too. It's been the best week of my life," revealed Ethan.

"Really?"

"Yes, really. Meeting you is the best thing that has ever happened to me."

"I feel the same way," admitted Avery. She continued, "I cannot believe it's been four weeks. It feels like I have known you forever."

"I know what you mean. Our holiday may be ending, but we have many more in front of us."

Avery turned to the lake and glanced across the glistening water. The moon cast its glow, illuminating the water. "A perfect end to a perfect holiday."

Ethan pulled her close and entwined his fingers through hers. They talked for hours, sharing stories and their wishes for the future, before heading back to the castle.

CHAPTER FOURTEEN

"Have you heard from Avery?" enquired Lucy.

"Nope, not a single word. I dropped her a message, but it hasn't been delivered. I'm guessing she turned her phone off. Or rather, Ethan has. I get she wants to enjoy her holiday, Lucy, but she is a different person around Ethan. The old Avery would have sent pics and checked in. It's like she can't do anything without his consent these days. I know damn well her phone being off is due to him. It's not something Avery would do. I can't forget the way he glared at me over lunch the other week. It was sinister. It's not normal behaviour. He views me as a threat."

Lucy furrowed her brows. "When is she due back?"

"Last night, I believe."

"Have you tried her again?"

"Yep. No response. Surprise, surprise!"

"Look, why don't you drive by her house and see if she's home?"

"I was thinking the same. Do you want to come with me?" pleaded Avery.

"I can't. I have a nail appointment in an hour. Call me with an update, though."

"Sure. I won't be surprised if Ethan answers the door!"

It was only a short drive to Avery's home. Willow saw a black 4x4 on the drive. Huffing to herself, she pulled up behind it and climbed out. The curtains in the living room were twitching. She rapped on the door. She could hear footsteps and chatter. The door flung open.

"Willow! We weren't expecting you," greeted Ethan, sporting a sinister grin.

"I wasn't aware I needed to book an appointment to see my best friend," retorted Willow.

Ethan's mouth snapped shut. An uncomfortable silence ensued. Then Avery appeared from the living room.

"Willow! Why are you standing on the doorstep? Come in."

Ethan's eyes followed Willow into the house. His jaw tightened. He closed the door behind them and headed into the kitchen, obviously annoyed.

Willow enveloped Avery in a tight hug. "How was your holiday?"

Avery sat down on the sofa and patted the seat beside her. "Sit down."

Willow sat beside her and caught Ethan glaring at her from the doorway. Ignoring him, she turned to Avery. "Tell me all about it."

Avery left no stone unturned.

Willow saw the happiness radiating from Avery's face. Her cheeks were glowing as she relayed her adventures, while intermittently glancing at Ethan, who was never more than a few feet away. It was clear to Willow that Avery was completely under Ethan's spell.

"It sounds amazing. I missed you, though. I left a few messages, but they weren't delivered.

"Ah, yes, Ethan thought it was best to live in the moment and turn off our phones. I only used it to take a few photos. Oh, that reminds me, he still has my phone. Just a moment."

Ethan speedily backtracked into the kitchen and sat on the stool.

Avery stepped into the hallway. "Ethan, can you pass me my phone, please?"

Avery stepped back into the living room and sat beside Willow. Ethan followed shortly after with her phone in hand. "Here you go. I forgot all about it."

Willow's eyes studied Ethan's face. His eyes locked on hers and bore into her. Intimidated, Willow turned away and continued talking to Avery, who had not noticed the uncomfortable, silent exchange between them.

"I'm sorry I've not been in touch. It was selfish of me. I should have sent you a text, at the very least. I've been a shitty friend lately."

Willow offered a warm, forgiving smile. "Hey, forget about it. Now, show me those pics of the castle. It sounds beautiful."

Ethan remained in the kitchen, his mood percolating silently while the girl's laughter echoed through the house. He leapt from the stool and paced the floorboards. Finally, he turned on his heel and burst into the living room, interrupting the conversation.

"I'm sorry, but don't forget we are going to lunch, Avery?"

Avery's eyes darted to Ethan. "Lunch?" she questioned.

Ethan looked her straight in the eyes while nodding his head. "Yes, we talked about it briefly last night. You must have forgotten."

"I'm sure we did. Sorry, it slipped my mind. I was tired when we got home from the long drive." She turned to Willow. "Sorry, it seems I have a lunch date! How about I drop by your house tomorrow and we can have lunch?"

Willow stood up. She ignored Ethan, who stood his ground, remaining firm by Avery's side with his arm around her shoulder.

He placed a fake smile on his face. "It was lovely to see you again, Willow. Come on, I will see you out so Avery can get ready for lunch."

Willow kissed Avery on the cheek and side-stepped past Ethan. Ethan swiftly followed behind.

"Willow?"

Willow spun around sharply.

"I didn't want to say anything just now when Avery was making lunch plans with you for tomorrow. But she won't be able to make it. I have arranged a surprise for her."

Willow took one step closer to Ethan and looked him square in the face. "That's convenient. If I didn't know any better, I'd swear you were trying to come between us. But of course, that is a ridiculous idea, don't you think?" She left her words hanging in the air, smiled, turned on her heel and headed for her car. She climbed in and then looked back. Ethan was still on the doorstep, glaring at her. An icy chill travelled down her spine. She shook off the shiver, started the engine, and sped away.

CHAPTER FIFTEEN

*A*lthough Willow and Avery messaged each other from time to time, it had been weeks since they had caught up face-to-face. Willow walked into the *Old Joint Stock* pub and scanned the room for Avery. A smile raised on her face when she caught sight of her sitting in the booth at the back of the room. Avery stood up and rushed over to greet her with a warm hug. "It's so good to see you. It's been too long. I'm sorry we never got to meet for lunch as planned all those weeks ago."

"I can't say I wasn't disappointed. But I totally understand. It was out of your hands. Now, what are you drinking?" Willow asked.

"I got here early and bought myself a chardonnay."

"Okay. I'm just going to order an orange juice. I'm driving."

Avery headed back to the booth.

Willow squeezed through to the front of the bar. The lunch time crowd was filling up the pub.

"Hey Willow," shouted Jacky from the far side of the bar.

Willow smiled as her favourite waitress pushed her way through the crowds over to her. "How are you?"

"I'm okay."

Jacky raised a curious brow. "You don't look okay. You know where I am if you need to vent," she offered.

"Thanks Jacky." Willow watched as Jacky headed to a nearby table of office workers and took their orders. She'd warmed to Jacky instantly, the first time they'd met. She fetched herself a drink and joined Avery.

"Can we talk candidly, Avery?"

"Of course, always. What's up?"

Willow circled the rim of her glass for a moment while pondering on the right words to impart.

"Willow?" pressed Avery.

"Sorry. It's just that I am worried about you."

"Me? What on earth for?"

"Come on, Avery. Since you got involved with Ethan, we barely talk anymore. Your phone is off more than it's on. Which is weird. When it is on, you either leave me on *read* or reply a day or so later. What the hell is that all about?"

Avery reached for her wine and took a large gulp. She searched Willow's concerned face. "I know I have neglected our friendship. And for that, I am sorry. Ethan is very intense and likes us to spend time alone together. He is not much of a social bunny. To be honest, that suits me perfectly. I am not one for all those big dinner parties and social get-togethers. That is why Ethan and I are perfect for one another. We are the same in some ways. Yes, I know he can be intense, but that's just who he is."

Willow shook her head, annoyed. "Look, you will not like what I have to say, but I'm going to say it, anyway. Ethan is controlling you. Who you can see and when you can see them. If you think about it for a minute, you'll see that I'm right. Every time we arrange to see each other, he either turns up unexpectedly with some sort of excuse to warrant his unannounced appearance or arranges something special for you both on the same day, feigning forgetfulness about your prearrangements. Coincidence much, don't you think?"

Avery's face sharpened. She stood up, reached for her glass, and drank down the rest of the wine, then headed to the bar to order another. Willow waited anxiously, knowing she had upset her friend. Avery returned with two large glasses of wine.

"Willow. You are my best friend. My only real friend. You more than anyone should understand how important Ethan is to me. I have never had a full-blown relationship before. Not like this, anyway. My only other meaningful relationship was over three years ago. Ethan is the one. You are wrong about him. Those things you said are pure coincidence, that's all. You don't know him as I do. He is the kindest and most thoughtful person I have ever met." Avery paused; an uncomfortable silence hung in the air. Avery turned to Willow, "I was going to wait to tell you, but I think now is as good a time as any. Ethan and I are moving in together!"

Willow's jaw dropped. Before she could react, Ethan entered the bar. Avery stood up and waved him over.

Willow raised her brows and glared at Avery. "Here he is, right on cue."

Avery ignored her and shuffled over to make room for Ethan.

Ethan approached their table with the confidence of a lion. "Willow! Good to see you again," he greeted plastering a fake smile on his face.

"Hello, Ethan. I wasn't expecting you to join us!" She turned to Avery and held her gaze, hoping for an explanation.

Ethan noticed the awkward moment and interjected, while focusing his eyes on Avery. "I'm sorry, love. I know you said three p.m. but my meeting finished early. It seemed fruitless driving home only to have to come back to pick you up. I hope you don't mind?"

Avery planted a kiss on his cheek. "Of course not. It makes complete sense. I shared our news with Willow."

They both turned to Willow. Willow forced a smile. "It's great news. If you are sure that's what you want, Avery. You have only been together three months."

Avery's brows snapped together. "Of course, it is. When Ethan first suggested we move in together, it was a little scary. Especially since I only bought my home three months ago. But now, I cannot wait. We talked everything through, and we are going to rent out my house. Ethan is taking care of all that for me. I wouldn't have a clue where to start."

Willow realised that she had lost Avery to Ethan. She knew that he was doing his best to isolate her. And there was nothing she could do about it until Avery, saw him for who he was. *I will be here for you, Avery when you need me. And I have this awful feeling you will need me in the future.*

Willow eased herself out of the booth. "Sorry Avery, I must dash. I need to pick Lucy up from the nail salon," she lied.

"Aww, can't you stay for one more drink?"

"Sorry. I would if I could." She caught Ethan smirking and shook her head in disgust. Then left. Willow was incensed when she reached her car. *I could've wiped that smirk off his smug face,* she raged.

She climbed in and called Lucy.

"Hey, are you home?"

"I'm heading home, now. Why what's wrong?"

"I seriously need to vent, Lucy. I will see you at home shortly."

"Sure. Do you want me to grab you a sandwich en route?" Lucy asked. "I am getting myself one."

"No thanks, I'm way to upset to eat. See you back at the house."

The more Willow thought about Ethan, the more she knew he was trouble. He made it near impossible for her to spend any time alone with Avery. His arrogant smirk told her all she needed to know. He knew exactly what he was doing. He was intentionally isolating Avery, and she didn't have a clue at all. *For God's sake, wake up Avery!*

Willow pulled up in the drive. Lucy was already home. She locked up her car and headed into the house.

Lucy appeared from the kitchen with half a sandwich in her mouth. "What the hell has happened?"

Willow threw her bag down on the chair and began pacing the tiled floor.

"Ethan, that's what's wrong. He infuriates me. I knew he would turn up uninvited today. It took me ages to get Avery alone. It was supposed to be a girls' lunch. I had a feeling Ethan would turn up, and he did."

Lucy's brows drew together. "You're kidding, right?"

"I wish I were. Weirdly, he turned up just after I unloaded my thoughts on Avery. Telling her he keeps turning up with excuses each time we have met up. Then he appeared on cue. What is wrong with him? What is he so afraid of?"

"Look, Willow, as your sister, I'm advising you to take a step back. I agree this is a very odd situation that Avery has found herself in. But if she won't acknowledge it, then there's not much you can do about it right now."

"I can't just walk away and give up on my best friend. Avery has no clue what she is getting involved with. She's so naïve. He is bad news, Lucy. It was me that encouraged her to go on a date with Ethan. I feel responsible. You should have seen the smug look on his face. He knew exactly what he was doing, and Avery was completely oblivious. Her love blinds her to him."

"I suggest you keep an eye on her from a distance, then," Lucy suggested.

"Don't make it too obvious to Ethan. We know nothing about him. Do some digging and see what turns up. Why don't you call that guy you went on a couple of dates with a while back. He knew Ethan, right?"

"Yes, but it would be awkward calling him now. I turned down a third date with him."

"Did he say anything about Ethan on your dates?" pressed Lucy.

"Not really. He is a client of Ethan's, not a friend. There was one thing he said, though. I paid no attention to it. He said it surprised him Ethan was dating again."

Lucy raised a curious brow. "Well, didn't you ask why?"

"No. The waiter turned up with our order and our focus turned to the food. I forgot about it until now. Our paths have crossed in town once or twice. He gets his coffee from the same coffee shop as me."

"Perfect. Well, next time you see him, strike up a conversation, and ask him about Ethan."

Willow shook her head. "I don't like it at all. But I'll do it. I need to know what Dillon meant."

Willow reached into the cupboard for a glass and took a carton of juice from the fridge. "Do you want one?"

"No, thanks."

Willow continued. "Other than that, there is little I can do. I just pray Avery will wake up soon. I have a bad feeling about Ethan that I can't shake off."

Lucy placed a comforting hand on Willow's arm. "And as her best friend, just be there for her when she needs you. You have already gone beyond the call of friendship. Avery does not know how lucky she is to have you as a friend."

"I guess. But that's what friends do. Anyway, what if I ask Jackson to speak to her? Avery and Jackson were always close. He had a way with her that no one else did."

"Mmm, I'm not sure that's a good idea. Jackson has enough on his plate. It may make things worse and push Avery further away."

Willow pondered Lucy's words for a moment. "Well, I'm going to ask Jackson, sound him out, and see if he will call her. It's not out of the ordinary. Jackson is her close friend, after all. He's just as worried about Avery as we are."

"It's your call, Willow. But don't say I didn't warn you if it backfires."

Willow huffed, reached for her phone, and called Jackson. It took forever for him to answer.

"Hey Willow, what's up?"

Lucy shook her head and left the room.

"I need a favour, Jackson."

"Sure. What is it?"

"Can you call Avery for a friendly chat? Ethan is proving to be a control freak. Avery has completely submitted herself to him. I can barely get her alone. When I arrange something, Ethan turns up. It's weird. He does not like me, and he's always got Avery's phone. Something is off, Jackson. She barely calls and does not pick up her messages. Oh, and get this, she is moving in with him. She's barely known him five minutes."

"She's moving in with him?" Jackson gasped.

"Yep. Can you believe it?"

"Well, no, I can't!"

Jackson paused.

"Jackson, you still there?"

"Yes. Sorry. Look, Avery, I'm not sure what it is you expect me to say to her. Ethan's true colours will surface, eventually. No one can keep up a false pretence permanently."

Avery sighed. "Can't you just call her up like you used to do, as her friend? Just say you're calling to say hi and catch up. See where the conversation leads you."

Jackson fell silent while pondering Willow's request.

"Jackson?"

"I'm still here. Okay, I will call her. But you owe me for this!"

"Thank you. Anything you want. I'm there," promised Willow.

"I have to collect Ruby. Speak soon." Jackson cut the call.

Lucy entered the kitchen. "Well, I got the jist of the call. I hope Avery does not cotton on that it's you who got Jackson to call her. She will be so pissed off with you, otherwise. But I get why you are doing it and I'll say it again, she's lucky to have you," admitted Lucy.

"Avery does not have anyone, Lucy. I have you, Jackson, and our parents. She has no family to turn to. And I know her well enough to know that if things went south, her pride would prevent her from reaching out for help. Ethan has love-bombed her, and she has fallen hard and fast."

"Well, like I said, keep an eye on her. All you can do is to be there for her if she needs you."

* * *

After putting Ruby to bed, Jackson called Avery. He waited patiently for her to answer, and he was about to cut the call when Ethan answered.

"Hello, Avery's phone."

"Hi, can I speak with Avery?"

The line went silent.

"Hello," pressed Jackson.

"I'm sorry. Avery is in the shower. Who can I say called?"

"Jackson."

A long pause ensued before Ethan repeated.

"Jackson?"

"Yes, that's what I said."

"Mmm, sure. Jackson. I'll let her know you called. Bye." Ethan cut the call leaving Jackson hanging.

Dumbstruck, Jackson glared at his mobile phone. "What the hell?"

He dialled Willow's number, and she answered immediately.

"Jackson?"

"So, I called Avery as you asked, and I think you're right. Ethan answered the phone. I realised he was not happy that I was calling her. He went silent briefly, before lightening his tone and telling me he would let Avery know I called. Then cut the call before I had a chance to say anything else."

Willow jumped in. "I told you something is off. He's not right in the head."

Jackson chimed in. "The trouble is, Willow, there's not a lot we can do at this point unless Avery reaches out. And right now, Avery thinks he is the best thing ever. But it was so strange how his tone changed like that. All you can do is to be there for her when she needs you and she will need you. Mark my words. It's all just a matter of time."

"Lucy said something similar, too. Thanks for doing that for me. I appreciate it."

"No problem. Keep me updated. If anything happens, let me know. I care about Avery too and don't want to see her getting hurt."

CHAPTER SIXTEEN

*E*than deleted Jackson's call and placed Avery's phone on the coffee table. His mood changed when Avery walked into the living room.

"Who was that on the phone?"

"A client," he snapped.

Avery searched Ethan's face. "What's the matter?"

Ethan responded sharply. "Nothing."

"It's just that you look like you received bad news or something."

Ethan snapped unexpectedly. "There's nothing wrong, okay? Stop pestering me."

Ethan's harsh response shook Avery. He had never spoken to her in that way. Shocked, she left the room and headed for the kitchen. Ethan swiftly followed behind, agitated.

"Don't walk away from me like that."

Avery averted his glare and pottered around the kitchen. Ethan walked up behind her, placed his hand on her shoulder, and spun her around to face him. "Maybe I should ask what's up with you?"

Avery pulled away and headed for the stairs. Ethan jumped in front of her. "Where do you think you're going? I'm not done talking."

"I don't want to get into a fight with you. What is wrong with you today?"

"A fight? Well, maybe you can explain what your relationship with Jackson is."

Avery fell silent, pondering his words. "Where has all this come from?"

Backtracking and smiling, Ethan said, "Just ignore me. I'm being ridiculous."

"No. You can't blurt something like that and expect me to ignore it."

Ethan paced the floor back and forth. "I am just curious to know if there was anything more than friendship between you and Jackson in the past?"

Avery's eyes widened. "Jackson is one of my closest friends and nothing more. He is a genuinely decent guy who has always had my back. Nothing more."

Ethan came close to Avery with a fixed smile on his face.

"I'm sorry. I just got a little paranoid. It was the way Lucy talked about him once. It's been stewing in my mind ever since. I just had to know. Forgive me?"

A smile reached Avery's eyes. "You are silly. Of course, I forgive you. You have nothing to worry about with Jackson. I promise. Jackson went through a tough time when he lost his wife. I was there for him, as I would be there for any friend."

"Have you confided in Jackson about your past?"

"Not in detail. I have revealed little about my past to anyone."

Avery paused. Ethan paced the floor anxiously.

"Ethan, I have touched on my past with you before. I know I have not talked about it in detail, but that's because it's too painful to visit. You have seen the scars I carry on my back. That should tell you all you need to know. I simply cannot trawl over the finer details. It traumatises me. Surely you can understand that."

Ethan studied Avery, noting her eyes tearing up. He walked over to her and brought her in close to him. "I love you, Avery. I want to understand what you went through, that's all. I want to know everything about you. Surely you can understand me."

Confused, Avery backed away. She didn't like the way the conversation was going. "I'm sorry Ethan, I can't have this conversation. I haven't even discussed it in detail with Willow, my friend, for almost seven years. Please, drop it."

Avery's unwillingness to divulge seemed to make Ethan more determined. "How can I help you on your bad days if I don't know what is causing your distress? If we are going to spend the rest of our lives together, then we should be open with each other."

Avery swept away her tears and turned to face Ethan. "Okay, you want to know about my past. You want to know how I suffered? Well, here it is. My mother was an alcoholic and she would lock me in my bedroom night after night. The window would be nailed shut, so I could not open it. During the summer months, it was almost unbearable. Strangers filled the house in the evenings. People my mother brought back from the pub. Loud music blared through the house into the early hours of the morning on school nights. Strangers would attempt to come into my room. I would watch the door handle go up and down, fearing one night the door might open."

Ethan inched towards her and extended his hand. "Please don't," she said, stepping away and fighting back her tears.

Avery continued. "Eventually, social services placed me in a children's home. It was horrible. Children were mistreated. I was mistreated. My scars resulted from me trying to resist a sexual assault from one of the night duty staff. He singled me out. He beat me into submission and then beat me again. One night, I fought so hard and got away from him. I ran out of the building down the street before he caught up with me. He dragged me back, stripped me naked, and beat me with a studded belt. That's how I got the scars. He threatened me with solitary confinement and worse if I ever spoke up against him. He convinced me I would not be believed. I soon realised there were other members of staff doing the same to other children. He raped me several times during my time in the children's home. My mother already broke me before I arrived there. He stole from me the only thing I had left—my innocence." Without warning, Avery ran out of the room, up the stairs, and flung herself down on the bed and cried. Ethan left her alone for a while to give her the space she needed. Eventually he returned. Pushing the bedroom door open, he found her curled up on their bed in a foetal position.

"Avery?"

Avery couldn't speak. She buried her face further into the pillow as she whimpered like a hurt animal.

"Avery, I'm so sorry. I didn't mean to push you so hard on this. I didn't know things were that bad for you. I am speechless."

After a while, Avery unfurled and sat up. Her eyes were red and raw from the tsunami of tears drowning her eyes. "Now you know why I have never spoken about my past. It is what it is. Talking about it does not help the fact it happened. Talking about it forces me to relive the trauma inflicted upon me and that is what I find unbearable. For the last time, Ethan, it is too painful for me. You wanted to know, and now you do. Please don't ask me about my past again."

Avery climbed off the bed to go wash her face, leaving Ethan to mull over her words.

After some time, Avery joined Ethan in the kitchen. "Do you want a coffee?" he asked.

She nodded. "Yes, thanks."

"How about I cook dinner tonight?"

Avery smiled. "That would be lovely."

Avery kissed him and then began searching for her phone. "Are you looking for this?" revealed Ethan, holding up her mobile phone.

"Ah, yes, thanks. I swear I'm getting forgetful."

"It happens to the best of us," commented Ethan with a wry smile.

After searching for Jax's number, Avery swiped to call. Eager to get back to work, she wanted to let her boss know she was ready. Jax's number sent her straight to voicemail.

Ethan was curious. "Who are you calling?"

Avery placed her phone in her jeans pocket. "Jax. I need to sort out my next assignment with him. I'm due back to work soon, remember?"

Ethan's mood switched instantly. "Why do you need to go back at all? I earn enough for both of us. I want to take care of you."

"I need to work, Ethan. It's what keeps me sane. I do the job that I do, as much for me as the families I help."

"But two months away? It's too long. Please, Avery, give us a bit more time," he pleaded.

Avery stared at her phone and then placed it down on the table. "I guess a little more time won't hurt. But I will go back eventually," she reminded then grabbed her coffee and took it into the living room. Ethan's brows snapped together as her last words took root in his mind.

CHAPTER SEVENTEEN

*A*lmost a year had passed since Avery moved in with Ethan. Willow barely saw her anymore. The odd text message and a couple of lunches were all Avery could manage. Willow's detective work had revealed nothing about Ethan. Apart from his registered company, her search found very little. She hadn't seen Dillon in the coffee shop again. Avery was in too deep, and she would not hear a wrong word spoken about Ethan. A huge rift formed in their friendship, but Willow refused to give up.

To Willow's surprise, she bumped into Dillon in town while shopping for a birthday gift for Lucy. Dillon smiled and made his way over to her. "Hey, how you doing?" he asked.

"I'm good. Shopping for a birthday present. How are you?"

Dillon swept his hair back off his face. "Busy as always. I'm guessing you heard my company parted ways with Ethan?"

Surprised, Willow shook her head. "No, I hadn't heard. I have seen little of Avery recently. What happened?"

"Professional differences. Look, it's cold out here. Fancy a coffee for old-time's sake?" suggested Dillon.

"Yes. Why not?" shivered Willow.

They headed into the coffee shop and Dillon ordered two lattes and sat down. Willow looked at Dillon thoughtfully.

"Okay, what's on your mind?"

Willow rolled her eyes. "You got me! The thing is, I have been worried about Avery. We know nothing about Ethan, and he comes off more than a tad controlling. I recall you saying to me once that it surprised you that Ethan was dating again. Why did you say that?"

Dillon put his coffee down and steepled his fingers beneath his chin. "You didn't hear this from me. All I know from a colleague is that Ethan was in a long-term relationship with a woman. It didn't end well." Dillon paused and took a sip of his coffee.

"What do you mean, it didn't end well?"

"All I know is that his girlfriend befell an unfortunate accident. She died. It devastated Ethan."

"What kind of accident?" pressed Willow.

"I know very little. Only she slipped and fell while they were on a hiking break in Loch Lomond, Scotland. It crushed Ethan."

"Scotland?!" repeated Willow.

"Yes. It was their favourite place to visit. That's why I was surprised he started dating Avery. Ethan is a very private man. He does not discuss his personal life with anyone and certainly not clients. I heard it from a colleague some time ago."

Willow fell silent while she tried to process Dillon's revelations. She sipped her coffee slowly and then glanced over at Dillon. "Thank you for sharing that with me."

"Hey, no problem. Hope it answers a few questions for you. That's why Ethan is the way he is. I guess you can't blame him. He's been through a lot."

Willow nodded reluctantly. "Sure. That must be it."

Dillon finished his coffee and stood up. "I must go. I have somewhere to be. It was lovely bumping into you again."

Willow stood up, too. "It was lovely to see you, too. Maybe we should do this again sometime?"

Dillon looked surprised. "Really?" I could have sworn a third date was out of the question!" he teased.

"Maybe a third date doesn't sound so bad after all!" she winked.

"Okay, Willow Forbes. How about we keep it simple? A coffee house date, same time, same place, next week?"

"It's a date!" she agreed.

"Okay, I really must go now. You have my number if you change your mind," finished Dillon, turning on his heel and heading for the door.

Willow sat back down to finish her coffee. Dillon's words ran through her mind like a steam train. *Was it an accident, though? And Scotland! That's where he took Avery...*

CHAPTER EIGHTEEN

"Come on, Jackson, answer your phone!" Willow said aloud.

"Hey, Sis, what's up?"

"I have some news on Ethan."

"Well, spill then?"

"Ethan's last girlfriend died. A tragic accident. But get this. It happened while they were holidaying in Loch Lomond, Scotland. Coincidence much!"

"You're kidding, right? Isn't that where he took Avery?"

"Yes! That's what's so strange about it."

"Hell no. This is too weird."

"Exactly my thoughts! But the weirdest thing I take from this current info is that they were hiking alone when she fell? I mean, come on, what are the chances? Suspicious or what?"

"I hear what you're saying. But it must have been officially declared an accident. Otherwise, if he had anything to do with it, surely, he'd be in prison."

"Maybe. But it's not beyond the realm of possibility, right?"

"I guess. I know Ethan's off. And I don't like him at all. But do you think he's capable of offing his ex-girlfriend? It just seems a bit much, Willow."

"I know. I'm probably reaching. As you said, if he had anything to do with it, he'd be in prison. I need to take a step back. But not before I do a wellness check on Avery and satisfy myself."

"Sounds like a good idea. Call me when you finally get hold of her."

"I will. Speak soon. Give Ruby a big hug for me."

* * *

After weeks of pestering, Avery agreed to meet Willow for lunch at her house. Willow clarified that Ethan was not welcome, and Avery assured her she would come alone.

Willow prepped a light lunch for them and chilled the wine. She spun around when the doorbell rang and dashed to open it.

Willow's lips curled up on the sight of Avery, and she enveloped her in a hug. "It's so good to see you. I've missed you," admitted Willow.

"I've missed you too."

Avery stepped through the hallway. Willow tried not to show her shock at Avery's waif-like appearance. She'd lost so much weight since they'd last met. Avery's shoulders hunched forward and her cheeks were scarily hollow.

"Come through to the kitchen. I've prepared lunch for us."

Avery followed Willow into the kitchen and sat down at the table positioned by the window overlooking the garden. Willow placed the platter on the table along with the salad bowl. She studied Avery as she glanced out of the window. She looked like a shadow of her former self. Willow noted the red marks on the side of Avery's neck that she had attempted to cover with a polo neck jumper. She forced a smile on her face, knowing she needed to tread carefully. She didn't want to upset Avery and encourage her to leave early.

"How've you been?" Willow asked.

Avery turned away from the garden and focused her attention on Willow. "I had the flu recently and I'm still recovering," Avery averted Willow's curious gaze and lowered her eyes.

"I thought you looked thinner. That'd be why then," responded Willow.

It became painfully obvious to Willow that she needed to drive the conversation. Avery appeared meek and lost almost disconnected.

"Are you happy, Avery?"

Avery turned away from Willow. A long silence ensued.

"Avery?" Willow pressed.

Avery stood up and reached for a tissue off the countertop, then turned to Willow. "I sold my house," she blurted.

"Oh, Avery. You didn't."

"I've been meaning to tell you. I was sad about it. But Ethan said it was for the best as our tenants left to buy their own house. It was sitting empty for a while. Ethan took care of everything. I wanted to keep it. But Ethan was right. It needed to be sold. I didn't make much on the sale. House prices have dipped a lot this year. But I got my deposit back and a little more." Avery paused and swiped a tear from her cheek before continuing. Willow hated to see her friend like this, she reached across the table and placed her hand on top of Averys'.

"I never really got to enjoy my house and I feel sad about that. But please, don't tell Ethan I said that. He is so sensitive and would read more into it."

Willow shook her head. "Of course not. Your feelings are justi-fied. Of course, you feel that way. You never got to enjoy it. And you worked so hard for that house. It was your childhood dream to own your own home. I wish I'd known. I could have helped you find a tenant."

"It wouldn't have made a difference. Ethan was adamant it needed to be sold."

"Of course, he was," blurted Willow.

Willow left the table and retrieved the wine from the fridge, poured two glasses, and handed one to Avery.

"Thank you. I've missed you, Willow. It's just that Ethan is so intense. I don't like to upset him." Avery lowered her eyes.

Willow noted Avery's hand tremble as she held the glass. "Avery, are you okay? It's just me and you, here. Ethan will never know what we talked about. You can trust me. I promise."

Willow allowed her words to linger in the air. She remained silent giving Avery the time to ponder. After some thought, Avery locked eyes with Willow.

"You promise?"

Shocked at Avery's response, she frantically nodded her head. "Promise!"

Avery took a deep breath. "Ethan changed after we moved in together. It was the trivial things at first. Whenever I was on the phone with my boss, Jax, he would be in listening range and then quiz me on the conversation afterwards. Then my phone would go missing at crucial times, like when I needed it to call Jax about work and even you. One time, I went to report it missing and he stopped me, assuring me it would turn up. And then it would turn up as if by magic. Then it got worse. Jax would call my phone and Ethan would delete the call or messages before I saw them. It would be days before I found out. Of course, when confronted by Jax about why I was not responding to calls and messages, it shocked me. I made up some lie and thankfully he bought it."

Infuriated, Willow shook her head. "You should have reached out to me. If only to vent."

"I know. I thought about it. But I stopped myself. I didn't want to burden you."

"Avery, you could never burden me. You are like a sister to me. Your problems are my problems, remember? That's what we always told each other."

Avery swiped the tears tumbling down her cheeks. "I

confronted Ethan about it and asked if he had deleted my messages and he got so angry with me for even suggesting it. But I know he did it. Because I got a paper statement from my mobile provider and the calls were there when Jax said they were. I didn't confront Ethan further. But it unnerved me. He gets quite angry, Willow. But I know he loves me, and fears losing me. That's all. He has separation anxiety. It occurred after losing his parents. He is just afraid that something will happen to me."

"Avery, you cannot make excuses for his behaviour. It's wrong what he is doing. He is isolating and manipulating you. The saddest part of what you have told me is selling your house. That was your independence, somewhere you could go back to if circumstances warranted it."

"I know. But I didn't have a choice. Or at least it felt like it at the time. Ethan gets into my head and then I feel guilty for challenging him. Like I'm being difficult or something."

Willow knew she had to choose her words carefully. The last thing she wanted was to scare Avery off now she had her confidence. "Just know, anything you share with me will remain between the two of us. If ever you need to reach out to me for any reason, night or day, then please do. I worry for you, Avery. I know you love him, but this relationship is toxic on multiple levels. I don't see it getting better for you."

Avery stood up and checked her phone, noting three missed calls from Ethan. Her entire stance changed.

"I better go. Thanks for lunch. Sorry I spent the entire time whinging. It's nothing to worry about. I'm just being dramatic." She hugged Willow, picked up her bag, and headed for the door.

"Avery?"

Avery spun around. "Anytime, and I mean, anytime, okay?"

Avery offered a weak nod and left Willow speechless on the doorstep. Willow called Jackson's number, and to her amazement, he answered straight away.

"Hey, Willow."

"Jackson, I got Avery on her own today. She came over for lunch. You should have seen her. A shadow of her former self, exceptionally thin, and even her cheeks were unhealthily hollow. Avery said she had flu recently, and that was the reason. But I know she's lying."

"You need to make her see, Willow. Or it won't end well. Ethan has complete control over her. He is preying on her weakness and vulnerability."

"I know that. I got her to confide in me a little. She sold her house. It shocked me. Avery said that Ethan handled the sale, and it was his idea. I think he made her feel guilty for holding on to it. My theory is this, he wants to make sure that Avery is reliant on him in every way. By stripping her of independence, he gains full control of her under the guise that he is taking care of her."

"Wow! You have really thought this through, Sis. You know better than me. You see Avery more than I do. All I do know at this point is we need to encourage her to break away from Ethan. It won't be easy though. Remember, she loves him and that is why she is making excuses for him. Avery does not deserve this. Of all the people she could have met, why did it have to be him?"

Willow jumped in. "I will keep reaching out to her and let her know we are always here for her. Whatever's going on in that house can't be good. I have never seen Avery look so worryingly thin. But like you said, we must be careful. Avery is extremely fragile right now."

"If things take a turn for the worse, call me straight away and I will be up there in a flash. I will see if I can unearth any information on this Ethan guy," finished Jackson.

"Thanks, Jackson. Bye for now."

CHAPTER NINETEEN

*A*very loaded the washing machine and began preparing lunch. The kitchen door swung open, and Ethan stood glaring at her in the doorway. His hands balled into fists. He expelled a harsh breath and inched forward.

Avery didn't turn around, choosing to ignore him. Ethan's eyes bore through her as she continued to prepare dinner. Before she knew it, Ethan had her arm in a firm grip and then he spun her around to face him.

"Don't do that, Avery."

Avery tried to avoid his eyes, to no avail. He gripped her head with both hands and turned it to face him. "I said, don't!"

Avery lowered her eyes and trembled.

"Where is your phone?" he demanded.

"I'm not sure. Maybe it's on the coffee table in the living room," she lied.

"No. It's not. Now, where is it?"

Avery tried to free her arm from his grip, but Ethan gripped harder. "Fetch me your phone *now, Avery*."

He released his grip on her arm, allowing her to scurry out of the kitchen. Ethan trailed close behind her. Avery climbed the stairs to their bedroom, knelt and retrieved her phone from under the bed, and passed it to Ethan.

Anger dominated Ethan's face. He swiped the phone from her hand and turned it on. Two messages from Willow flashed across the screen. His eyes widened as he read the messages of concern from Willow. He threw the phone down on the bed and inched closer to Avery. His hands circled her neck, and he tightened his grip.

"How long have you been visiting Willow behind my back?" he roared.

Avery shrunk into the wall. "It was just a couple of lunches. She's my best friend, Ethan. I miss her."

Ethan raged. "She is not a good friend, Avery. How many times do I have to tell you? She is trying to come between us. I didn't want to have to tell you this, but well... you leave me no choice," he loosened his grip on her neck and took a step back.

Avery rubbed her neck and flinched back from him.

"What are you flinching for?"

Avery remained silent. She knew when he was like this that the best thing she could do to prevent the situation from escalating was to be compliant.

"Why do you do this, Avery? You cause this tension between us—you alone. You know that, right?"

Avery avoided his glare.

Ethan inched closer. "*I said, right?*"

Avery cowered into the wall and nodded. "I'm sorry, I don't mean to upset you."

As if someone had flicked a switch, Ethan's mood softened. "There is a reason Willow has been so determined to break us up. You see, in the beginning of our relationship, Willow came on to me."

Avery shook her head. "No. She would never betray me like that."

Ethan grimaced. "And yet she did. I would not lie about something like that. I never told you because I knew it would hurt you. I knew how much Willow meant to you. I was trying to protect you. But now you can understand why I was so keen for you to keep your distance from her. And it wasn't the first time either. I'm sorry, Avery. But I am tired of looking like the bad guy. It's time you realised Willow is not the great friend she purports to be. Maybe now you can understand why I have been a little intense where Willow is concerned."

Avery's eyes filled up. She didn't know whom to believe anymore. Ethan left the room, taking her phone with him. She slid down the wall and crumpled into a heap, running every scenario through her mind, and concluded there was a possibility Ethan was right.

From the beginning, Willow had a problem with Ethan. Before she even knew him properly. It explains his odd behaviour regarding Willow. But it seems so out of character for Willow. This is a nightmare. I trusted her and shared my problems with her. And she knew all along why Ethan was aloof with her. Maybe that's why he got so paranoid over the months, worried Willow would try to break us up. It would certainly explain his behaviour. I need to speak to Willow, she concluded.

Avery found Ethan in the kitchen. He turned around. "I need to drop by the office. I have a client meeting. When I'm done, I thought we could go out for dinner. My way of saying sorry for my outburst and ruining lunch. How does that sound?"

Avery shook her head. "I'm not feeling up to going out. Can we stay home?"

"Of course. Why don't you cook us dinner instead?" he suggested.

"Sure," Avery agreed.

"Maybe you could cook my favourite meal. You know how happy that makes me. Oh, and put on the blue dress with the belt. It's one of my favourites."

Avery offered a poor nod and watched him as he grabbed his

keys off the hallway console table and leave. She waited for Ethan to pull off the driveway, ensuring he was gone before searching the house for her mobile phone. *Where the hell has he put it?* She cursed. Her search was fruitless. She grabbed her bag and headed out the door. The drive to Willow's took less than fifteen minutes. She leapt from the car and rapped on Willow's door. Willow greeted her with surprise. "Avery! I wasn't expecting to see you today."

"Can I come in? I haven't got long. So, I will be quick."

"Of course."

Willow stepped aside and Avery burst into the hallway.

Willow noticed how upset Avery was, raising her brow while patiently waiting for Avery to speak.

"Avery, what's wrong? You're scaring me."

Avery paced the tiled floor anxiously. "Is it true? Did you come on to Ethan early in our relationship?"

Willow's brows drew together. "What the hell?"

Avery kept her focus on Willow.

"I cannot believe you even have to ask, Avery. For fuck's sake!"

"I had to. Ethan said that's why there is a rift between you two. And it would certainly explain a few things."

"He's wrong. I would never do that to you. I simply cottoned on to him early. He is bad news, Avery. And just in case it's another few months before I see you, I must say this: Ethan is not good for you. Answer me this, have you been able to make one independent decision since moving in with Ethan? By that I mean a decision that he did not encourage or discourage. Think real hard."

Avery sat down on the wooden bench at the bottom of the stairs defeated. Then looked up. "I'm sure I have. Today, yes, I am here, aren't I? Ethan doesn't know where I am right now. But I need to get home before he notices that I'm gone."

"Well, that you had to sneak out behind his back for fear of his reaction tells me all I need to know. And should alert you to your senses. Wake up Avery, before it's too late."

Avery rose to her feet, her face turned pale. "I just don't know

how to manage this right now. I love him, Willow. He is compli-
cated, yes. He sees you as a threat to our relationship. Rest assured,
I will question him about this. But I see no reason he would lie
about this either. So, you can understand my predicament? I am
caught between a rock and a hard place."

Willow snapped. "No, I can't. You have known me for a
quarter of your life, and you have known Ethan for five minutes.
Yet, you believed him, or you would not have landed on my
doorstep today. You would not have felt the need to ask me if his
statement was true. You should have instinctively known it
wasn't. But you are so blinded by your love for him, you cannot
see past his bullshit. And until you open your eyes to him, things
are going to get much worse for you, Avery. Mark my words.
Maybe you need to look up the word 'narcissist' because it is an
accurate description of Ethan. And you're the only one who can't
see it."

An uncomfortable silence ensued between them.

Willow continued. "I would never hurt you like that. Our
friendship is worth too much to throw away over a guy."

Avery turned away from her. "I don't know what or who to
believe anymore. You are both so convincing. I'm confused."

Willow saw the depleted look on Avery's face. "Please, just be
careful. Ethan has trust issues, and he's obsessive with you. It's
unhealthy for you both. The fact that he lied about this, tells me he
will do anything to break our friendship. And quite frankly, he's
doing a great job of it."

"I don't know who is lying right now, Willow. Try putting yourself in my shoes for one moment. My best friend and my fiancé are
at odds. I love you both, but one of you is lying to me. I don't know
who to believe right now. But I will talk to Ethan when he gets
home and try to set some boundaries. Don't be offended, but Ethan
looks at my phone sometimes. Don't leave me messages, okay? It
just sets him off. He sees your name and flips. If I don't answer the
phone, it's because I can't. I will call you back when I can."

Willow shook her head from side to side in frustration. "Okay. But can you hear yourself? It's insane, Avery."

"I know how it sounds. But I just want to keep the peace."

"No, Avery. You are navigating around his moods and bad temper. It's obvious he is physically abusing you. Have you looked at yourself in the mirror lately? You turned up here the other day with a polo neck on to hide the red marks around your neck. Yes, I saw them."

Tears cascaded down Avery's cheeks. Dumbstruck by Willow's words, she turned for the door.

Willow halted her. "Oh, before you go, Avery, I am heading to Croatia for two weeks with Lucy."

Avery didn't turn around. "I really must go now."

Avery swung open the door and exited.

Willow ran to the door and shouted after her. "Avery, I would never do anything to hurt you. You know that. Please tread carefully with Ethan. All is not right with him."

Avery didn't respond and continued to her car.

Willow watched with a sense of deep sadness as Avery drove off. A tense feeling circled her stomach. *This will not end well.*

CHAPTER TWENTY

*A*very's heart skipped a beat when she saw Ethan's car parked in the driveway. *What's he doing at home?* Before she reached the front door, a lone magpie caught her eye. It was perched on the cypress tree outside the porch, staring at her. She paused and stared back. The magpie held her gaze for a moment before flying off.

Ethan flung open the front door and stood glaring at her. Intimidated, she lowered her eyes as she approached him.

"Where have you been?" he demanded.

Avery averted his haughty stare and attempted to walk past him into the house. He gripped her arm and halted her. "Not so fast. I asked you a question. Now, where the fuck have you been sneaking off to?"

Avery searched his face and saw nothing but anger etched into it. She knew she needed to handle him delicately when he was like this. She forced a smile.

"I went to the post office," she lied.

Ethan's grip tightened. He pulled her into the hallway and slammed the door shut.

"You're lying. I can always tell when you're lying to me. Now, I will ask you one more time, where have you been?"

Avery shuddered beneath Ethan's towering figure. Her eyes shimmered with tears, and she whispered, "I went to see Willow."

Ethan expelled a harsh breath. He released his grip on her arm and began pacing the wooden floor angrily. Avery shrank into the wall, rubbing her arm. Fear enshrouded her. Avery tried to anticipate his next move, but nothing could have prepared her for what came next. Ethan spun around, raised his fist, and punched her cheek. She toppled, hitting the floor full force, and clipping the back of her head on the marble console table. She yelped in pain and writhed on the floor, caressing her cheek. Her phone slipped from her hand and slid across the floor. Ethan grabbed it as Avery scurried into a corner and cradled her arms around her legs, pulling them in close to her chest.

Ethan scrolled through her phone and then threw it at her. "Why did you make me do this? This is all your doing. You know that, right?"

Avery did not look up. Her head rested on her knees as she whimpered from the pain.

"Don't ignore me. You made me do this. All because you lied. Now what I want to know is why the fuck you felt the need to lie to me, and don't make me ask you twice."

Avery knew she could not win either way. It was only a matter of moments before he hit her again. Her eyes flooded with tears, and she could already feel her cheek swelling.

She glanced up at him. "I needed to confront Willow."

Ethan raged. "So let me get this straight. You needed to confront Willow about what I revealed to you?"

Avery nodded nervously.

"And I am guessing she denied it?"

"Yes," she said, shifting her gaze from him.

"Of course, she did. What did you expect, a full confession? Are you wilfully stupid? You went behind my back, Avery, because you clearly doubted me."

Ethan crouched in front of Avery. Avery winced. To her surprise, his face softened. He placed his hand over her cheek. He leaned forward and placed a soft kiss over the swelling.

"I love you."

He stood up and extended his hand. Avery's body shivered as she climbed to her knees and placed her hand on his. "Let's get you a cold press for the swelling."

Avery sat down on the stool at the centre island, too afraid to speak, unsure of what Ethan would do next. His unpredictable nature frightened her. Ethan dabbed her face with ice wrapped in a flannel.

"That should control the swelling. Let's look at your head."

Ethan studied the minor cut on the side of her head. Blood trickled out slowly. He walked over to the kitchen cupboard, flung open the door, reached for the first-aid kit, and retrieved gauze and plaster to hold it in place. Then took some cotton wool and ran it under the tap. Avery didn't move an inch. Ethan made his way over to her and tilted her head to the side. "Let's get this cleaned up. Luckily, it's just a clip and no lasting damage was done." He cleaned the wound and then dressed it. "There, all done. Feel better?"

Avery nodded. "Thank you."

"Now, I suggest you lie down on the sofa. I will cook dinner for us. How does that sound?"

Avery searched his face. His anger dissipated and the Ethan she fell in love with had returned. The Ethan that surprised her with an incredible first date. She offered a half smile, nodded, and climbed off her stool.

"Hey, not too fast now. You took quite a blow to your head and face."

At that moment, she knew she was in far too deep.

CHAPTER TWENTY-ONE

*W*illow had not heard from Avery since she'd returned from Croatia with Lucy. She'd been back a few days and left several messages that were not delivered. On a whim, she visited Avery. She had to know that she was okay.

"Where are you going?" questioned Lucy, watching Willow zip up her boots.

"I must know if Avery is okay. I have a bad feeling. None of my messages have delivered to her. Her phone is constantly off. I tried calling and was sent straight to voicemail. I know this is all down to that narcissist, Ethan. He was bad from the get-go. God only knows what lies he's fed her while I've been away."

"I'm not sure you should go, Willow. Ethan sounds unpredictable. If he is as bad as you claim he is, then he may take your unannounced visit out on Avery. If I were you, I would call her boss and see if she has been at work recently. Then we can take it from there. I am as worried as you are. But we must be clever about this."

Willow nodded and began unzipping her boots. "You're right. I will call Jax and see what he says."

Lucy busied herself in the kitchen while Willow called Jax. She gazed out of the kitchen window and watched the cars drive by. She didn't notice Ethan's car parked by the curb farther down the road.

* * *

Ethan's eyes rested on Willow's car. He noted that Avery's car was not on the drive, and he smiled. *Well, at least Avery is telling the truth for once. She's not here.* He started his car and drove off.

* * *

Willow walked into the kitchen. Lucy spun around. "Well, what did Jax say?"

"You will not believe this. Avery has been off sick for months. She never returned to work following her extended leave. Jax has tried reaching out to her but has gotten a brief response. He said he has been receiving her sick notes, but she has not returned his calls recently. He's quite worried about her. I asked him what was wrong with her. He said her doctor signed her off with mental health issues. He needs to speak with Avery regarding her future with the company. To be honest, I'm surprised PCAB haven't replaced her already."

Lucy shook her head, confused. "That is not like Avery at all. I wonder why she never mentioned it the last time you spoke to her."

"I have no idea. I am worried about her, Lucy. This is bad. She loves her job with a passion. She would do nothing to jeopardise it. This is all Ethan's doing. He is controlling every aspect of Avery's life. What the hell can I do?"

Lucy paced the tiled floor while Willow poured herself a glass of water and drank it down in one. Willow turned to Lucy. "I have heard enough. I am going over there right now, and you are coming with me."

Lucy didn't need asking twice. They slipped on their trainers and left. The short drive to Ethan's house was an anxious one.

"I hope we are doing the right thing," Lucy said on the way.

"Me too. But I can't just ignore what's happening. Something is off. I would never forgive myself if anything happened to Avery, and I did not do everything I could to reach out to her."

"I get that. I support you all the way. But we must be careful too. We have no idea what Ethan is capable of."

Ethan's house came into view. His car was not on the drive, but Avery's was. Willow parked up behind it. Willow turned to Lucy. "Are you ready?"

"Yep. Let's do this."

They approached the front door and rang the bell. "I can hear footsteps inside," Willow said.

Willow and Lucy locked eyes. Willow shouted out. "Avery, it's Willow! I know you are in there. Open the door. I'm not leaving until I've seen you."

Silence ensued. To their surprise, the door clicked open. Willow eased the door wide open, and her jaw dropped at the sight of Avery.

"Oh, God, no. What happened to you?"

Avery turned away from their gaze. "It's not what you think. I slipped and fell down the stairs while hoovering the other day. I cracked my head and clipped the corner of my face. It looks worse than it is. All bruises and no substance."

Avery's words did not convince Willow. Lucy remained in shock, unable to speak. Avery's face was a mess and covered in bruises.

"I don't buy it. What the hell has Ethan done to you?"

Avery stepped back. "Why do you always think it's Ethan? He's right about you, always sticking your nose in where it does not belong. You can't be here, Willow. Please leave," she demanded.

Willow stood firmly, refusing to leave. She turned to Lucy. "This is insane. Look at her face."

"I see it. But there is nothing we can do if she refuses our help."

Avery chimed in. "Refuses help? You are not listening. I just told you what happened. It had nothing to do with Ethan."

"Okay, say I believe you and you are right. If I have nothing to worry about, why are you off work for your mental health?"

Avery raised her brows, shocked. "How do you know about that?"

"I called Jax. I was worried about you. You have your phone off all the time. You don't return my calls. What did you expect me to do—ignore it?"

Avery forced back her tears. "Please go, Willow. I know you mean well, but you're not helping me. Quite the opposite, in fact. Ethan is due home any second now, and you cannot be here when he arrives."

Lucy tugged Willow's arm. "Come on. There is nothing we can do."

Willow nodded in defeat. "Fine, we shall leave. But don't think for one minute I am buying any of this. It's bullshit, Avery, and you know it, too. Just know, if you need me, I am always here for you. I'm your friend, remember that."

Avery closed the door swiftly. She leaned against it, sliding to the floor in a crumpled heap, crying. She hated lying to Willow but could not risk Ethan seeing her on their doorstep afraid of the repercussions.

Lucy shook her head in frustration and returned to the car, followed by Willow.

"What are you waiting for? Drive!" pressed Lucy.

"That was so infuriating. Don't tell me that nothing is wrong in that house, Lucy."

"I agree with you. But like I keep saying, there is nothing we can do until Avery reaches out for help. She is clearly under his spell or something."

"There is no way she fell down the stairs. I reckon Ethan did it. I barely recognise her from the Avery I knew. It's clear that Ethan is physically abusing her."

"I agree. But Avery is in classic denial. The fact that she is making excuses for him tells me all I need to know: she fears him.

And until she opens her eyes to what Ethan is—a violent abuser—then there is very little that we can do, other than letting Avery know that line of communication between us is open and always will be. There will come a time when she reaches out to you, Willow. But we cannot force it, or she may retreat further."

Willow's face paled. "I hate this. I hate that I can't help her. How the hell did we get here, Lucy?"

"Ethan is a narcissist, and he is very manipulative. He knew Avery was vulnerable and naïve. I am guessing over time he's weaponised her weaknesses against her. That's what they do. Avery did not see him coming, that's for sure."

CHAPTER TWENTY-TWO

*A*very ended her call with Jax. Ethan inched closer, shaking his head. "You can't be seriously considering going back to work. I thought we had discussed this. I thought I had made my feelings crystal clear?"

"I need to, Ethan. I am drowning here. I need to get back to doing what I love. Surely you can understand that. Please, Ethan, I just need to work."

Ethan paced up and down the living room. "You won't be able to cope with the long hours. It will be too much for you. I say this because I care about you. And I would miss you if you went to Africa. I earn enough money for us both. There is no need for you to work. I want to take care of you. How many times do I have to tell you this?"

"I know. But I need this, or I will go insane. I have been cooped up in this house for too long. Jax needs me back at work, and I am ready. I already told him I will return next week. My first trip will only be for two weeks until I settle back into my role."

Ethan fumed. "NO. I can't allow you to do this. All that travelling is not good for any relationship. A month here, two months there. Can't you find a new job that does not require so much travelling? Maybe a little part-time job to satisfy your itch."

Avery turned away from him. "I don't want another job. I'm lucky I still have this one. I love my job and I need it. Please understand."

Ethan grabbed his wallet and stormed out of the house. Avery expelled a hefty breath and slumped down on to the sofa. *That went far better than I thought. I need to get away from him. I need to think this through. Getting out of the country through my work is the beginning. Then I can begin searching for somewhere else to live. Just keep your focus on that for now.*

A couple of hours later, Ethan stormed through the door. The smell of whisky emanated from his breath. Avery jumped up from the sofa. Ethan stumbled towards her.

"I have given us much thought. And I have decided you are not going to Africa. End of conversation." He tripped over the coffee table and steadied himself on the armchair.

"Get me a glass of water," he demanded.

Avery looked at him in disgust. She turned on her heel and headed to the kitchen. Before turning the tap, she felt Ethan's grip on her shoulder spinning her around. "I saw the way you looked at me. Who the hell do you think you are?"

He drew his hand up and clipped her cheekbone hard. Avery yelped and fell back against the kitchen cabinet. Ethan grabbed her by the hair, wrapped it around his hand, dragged her out of the kitchen and threw her down on the cold hallway floor.

"You will be going nowhere. I suggest you get in touch with Jax and explain to him you are not ready to go back to work."

Ethan left Avery crumpled on the floor. He made his way up the stairs, climbed into bed fully clothed, and passed out. Avery struggled to the living room and climbed onto the sofa, where she cried herself to sleep.

Avery woke up sometime later. The house now dark and deafeningly quiet. She brushed the tears from her face, cupped her cheek to ease the throbbing, and went into the kitchen. Filled with despair, she buried her head in her hands crying until there were no tears left. Eventually, she pulled herself together and felt more determined than ever to go to Africa. *Nothing is going to stop me. I must get away from him. Willow's right. If I don't, he is going to kill me one day, I'm sure of it. I must make Ethan believe that I'm not going. Then he will back off.*

When Ethan's feet pounded the bedroom floorboards, Avery almost jumped out of her skin. She rushed around the kitchen and started rifling through the cupboards.

Ethan appeared in the kitchen doorway. "What are you doing?"

"I'm making dinner. I thought we could talk over an enjoyable meal?"

Ethan studied her face for some time. Avery shifted nervously on her feet, fearing he could see through her lie.

Satisfied, he nodded. "That's a promising idea. I'm sorry I lost my temper. I just can't bear the thought of you leaving for so long. I fear the worst will happen. I worry. You know how I suffered when I lost my parents. I can't bear to lose you, too. I just want to take care of you."

Avery forced a smile. "I know that. So, I have decided not to go. That's the end of it. You're right, it would not be good for us."

Ethan beamed. "Now why couldn't you have come to that realisation at the start? Then I would not have been forced into losing my temper."

Avery kept a forced smile while prepping dinner. Ethan poured himself an orange juice while barely taking his eyes off her. "It's the right decision, you will see."

Avery nodded. "I will go to the office tomorrow and speak with Jax. I'm sure he will understand."

"That's my girl. You have made me extremely happy." Ethan left the kitchen. Avery stopped what she was doing, placed both hands down on the countertop, and expelled a harsh breath.

CHAPTER TWENTY-THREE

*A*very walked into Jax's office. He gasped at the sight of her. He stood up, his six feet towering over her. He brushed a slope of light brown hair from his face and walked from behind his desk to Avery.

"What the hell, Avery? That looks painful. Close the door." Jax pulled out a chair and extended his hand. "Take a seat."

"Thank you."

Jax sat down. He studied the bruises on Avery's face.

Avery broke the silence. "Thank you so much for everything. I didn't want to drag you into this. You could have said no, hell, you could have fired me. But you didn't. I can never thank you enough."

Jax searched Avery's desperate face. "You are one of my best project managers. Over the years, you have gone beyond for PCAB and me. Going abroad at short notice and staying long over your project term date. I need you as much as you need me. Let's call it *quid pro quo!*" He winked.

Avery smiled. "Thank you. As I explained on the phone, Ethan believes I'm here to hand in my notice. I need him to believe that I have done just that. It's the only way I will walk out of that house in one piece and leave for Africa. Once I have left, I will never return to him. Once Ethan realises that I have left, he will be furious. His anger will lead his actions. I fear even Willow may catch the brunt of his temper. He hates her with a vengeance."

Jax listened intently and then chimed in. "As I mentioned, I have a rental house on the opposite side of town that is currently empty. You can stay there for as long as you need to."

"Thank you. Ethan will check up on me in a day or two. He will want to know I handed in my resignation. So, expect a call from him. He always checks everything I do."

A look of despair crossed Jax's face. "Oh Avery, why didn't you come to me sooner?"

Avery swiped a tear escaping down her bruised cheek. "I didn't have the courage until now. Besides, for the longest time, I truly believed there was something wrong with me. I thought it was something I was doing wrong."

Jax shook his head in frustration. "You deserve so much better than him. If he calls me, I will let him believe you have left the company. Just make sure you get on that plane next week. Willow will be at the airport with your tickets. Did you bring your passport?"

Avery reached into her bag and retrieved her passport. "It took me forever to find it. Ethan hid all my documents. It's his assurance I will not leave him. I just pray he doesn't notice it has gone. Here you go. I'm just trying to stay one step ahead of Ethan."

"That was a wise decision. I can't imagine what it must feel like to be in your mindset right now. Just be safe. If you need me, call. And stay safe."

Avery stood up, walked around to Jax, and hugged him tightly. "Thank you. You don't know what this means to me."

Jax squeezed her arm. "I have a pretty good idea. Now get out of here!"

Avery left the building and crossed the road to where Ethan waited impatiently in his car. She climbed in and belted up. She didn't see Jax peeking through the blinds of his office window, shaking his head in frustration as Ethan pulled away.

"Well, what did Jax say?" Ethan demanded.

"Disappointed. But accepted my decision to leave. He tried to talk me out of it, but soon realised I'd made my mind up."

Ethan studied Avery's face. "It's for the best. You know that, right?"

"Yes, I know. I will find something local. But maybe in a few weeks. There is no rush."

"Exactly. It's not like you need to work. As I have said before, I earn enough for both of us. Besides, I like to come home to you cooking dinner and greeting me. I'm thinking of booking the castle in Scotland again. That was the best holiday we ever had. I want to recreate it. What do you think?"

Avery panicked. *It was as if he can read my mind and knows what I have planned. Don't be ridiculous, Avery!*

Nodding her head, she replied, "I think it's a lovely idea. But why not time it for our anniversary next month? It would be the perfect way to celebrate," she suggested.

"Sure, next month it is. I will get on to it later."

Avery sighed with relief. *I need to be careful. I cannot give him a reason to get suspicious.*

Ethan pulled into the driveway. Ethan took Avery's hand as they walked to the house and winked as he opened the door. "Let's go upstairs."

Avery's heart sank. Disgust and revulsion infused her. Forcing a smile, she placed her hand in his and he led her upstairs to the bedroom.

Ethan lay her down on the bed, removed her clothes and threw her dress to the floor. He studied her naked body for some time. Uncomfortable, she turned to the side. Annoyed, Ethan reached a hand up to her cheek and forced it to face him before removing his clothes. Trapped beneath his power, she feigned a smile, and grit her teeth as he entered her. She wanted to run.

She prayed it would end quickly. Ethan flipped her over onto her stomach. Avery gripped the bedsheet between her fingers while forcing back her tears. The pain of his brute force cut like a knife. It wasn't long before Ethan finished and climbed off her.

"I'm going for a shower. Get dressed." He reached for her dress off the floor and threw it at her, completely void of emotion. Once Ethan was in the shower, Avery hugged her dress close to her chest and broke down. Belittled and vulnerable, she shrank into a ball. Their love making had ceased months ago, replaced by one-sided, brutal sex that Avery dreaded. But refusing to comply brought her much worse.

CHAPTER TWENTY-FOUR

*A*very waited until Ethan left for work the next morning before grabbing her handbag and stepping outside. She double-checked the road in both directions before climbing into her car. She needed to be sure Ethan was not lurking nearby, something she knew he did from time to time to track her movements. Checking her watch, Avery concluded she had roughly three hours before he came home for lunch. Something she hated he did. Now, she looked forward to having something she once enjoyed and longed for since Ethan came into her life: A full day to herself. Living every day on a knife's edge had taken its toll.

She swerved onto Willow's drive, leapt out of the car, and ran up to the door. Before she could knock, Willow swung the door open, and Avery hurried into the hallway.

Willow hugged her tight. "How long have you got?"

"Three hours, tops. He always comes home for lunch. I will need to be back at least thirty minutes before he is due home."

"That's plenty of time," Willow said.

"I couldn't answer your call yesterday. Ethan was around. It's near impossible to have a private moment these days. He watches everything I do. I'm scared, Willow. If he ever finds out what I'm planning, well...I don't know what he will do. He is becoming more unpredictable by the day."

"He won't find out. There is no way he could know. You will be fine. When Jax called and told me everything, I was so relieved for you. I just had this horrible feeling circling inside about Ethan. The sooner you get away from him, the better. Working in Africa for two months is genius and Ethan will never suspect you are there as he thinks you left your job. Just make sure you get on that plane on Monday. Jax has arranged everything."

"I'll be there. Nothing will stop me from getting on that plane—nothing!"

"Okay, let's go to the bank. Did you bring all the necessary ID?"

Avery rifled through her bag and nodded. "Yes, I have it. I found where Ethan was hiding my documents. I'm scared he will find them gone before I get on that plane."

"You can't think about that or you will drive yourself mad over the weekend and give off suspicious vibes to Ethan. I'm guessing he rarely looks at them. He thinks they're hidden away from you."

"That's true. I'm just scared, Willow."

"I know you are. Hell, I would be too. But you got this, Avery. You will be free of him soon."

They headed for Westwick, an old coaching town, four miles away to avoid any possibility of bumping into Ethan. Avery's bank sat in the centre of the square.

"Would you rather I wait here?" said Willow.

"No, I need you with me," Avery insisted.

Willow offered a comforting smile and looped Avery's arm as they entered the bank.

"Hello, how may I help you today?" the cashier asked.

Avery handed over her ID. "I would like to make a transfer into this account and then close my account here, please."

The cashier picked up the card Avery handed to her and began tapping on her keyboard. Can I have your ID please?"

Avery retrieved her ID from her bag and slid it through the gap in the Perspex shield.

The cashier picked up Avery's ID, studied it and glanced at Avery. "You wish to transfer all of it?"

"Yes."

"May I ask why you are closing your account with us today?"

Avery glanced at Willow, and then back to the cashier. "New investment plans."

"Okay. Well, we will be sorry to lose you."

"So, just to clarify, you will transfer £25,430 today from your current account to the account of Miss Willow Forbes. Account number, 008945678?"

Avery nodded, "Yes."

"Just give me a minute, while I make the transaction and formally close your account."

Avery and Willow waited patiently. Avery rubbed her thumb and forefinger together, as she always did when she was anxious.

"Okay. That is all done for you, Miss Masters. Have a nice day." Avery took her documents, thanked the cashier, and left with Willow.

"I told you everything would be fine. If you were going to withdraw all that money in physical cash, well now that would have required an appointment and questions from the bank manager, with it being such a huge amount. High Street banks rarely have that amount of money in their vaults. You must phone ahead to arrange it. But transferring from one account to another is far simpler for them, no actual cash involved."

Avery turned to her friend. "Hey, Willow, thanks for doing this. There is no one I trust more. That money is all I have left in the world. Most of it was from the sale of my house and some from savings. I will need to buy a new house at some point."

"Well, you don't need to think about that right now. The most important thing is getting on that plane. You can't give Ethan any reason to suspect you. Just act normal over the weekend. No more or less than you always do," Willow advised.

"You're right. I have Jax's rental to move into when I get back. Willow, I'm so sorry for everything. You could have given up on me months ago and you didn't. I lost myself for a while and I'm sorry for that. I don't know how I will ever make it up to you."

"Stop right there. You have nothing to be sorry for. Like I would give up on my bestie!" assured, Willow placing her arm around Avery's shoulder as they walked.

"At least your money is safe now. Ethan can't take it away from you. You can rest easy knowing you have your job, and you are financially secure. Let's go for a coffee and cake across the square. We have plenty of time."

CHAPTER TWENTY-FIVE

*E*than arrived home on cue and found Avery in the kitchen preparing lunch. He stood silently in the doorway, watching her. Avery felt his eyes on her, but did not react, move, or turn around. She continued tossing the salad, using all her will to remain calm.

"What are we having today?"

Avery didn't turn around when she answered him. "Greek salad with ciabatta and hummus dips."

Ethan walked up behind her and spun her around. "Where's my kiss?"

The pit of her stomach turned. She placed a kiss on his cheek and continued plating their lunch. Ethan took off his jacket and hung it over the dining chair and sat down while Avery organised the plates on the table. She sat down opposite him and dressed the salad with pepper and sea salt.

"So, what have you been up to this morning?" Ethan shot a glance around the room. "Not cleaning, I see?"

Avery shuddered and lowered her eyes to her plate. "I had a

headache and lay down for a couple of hours until it wore off. Sorry."

"Oh, you poor thing. How are you feeling now?"

She glanced over the table at Ethan. "A lot better. Thanks."

"Good. I'm glad to hear it. I have a client coming over for dinner this evening and I need you to prepare one of your special meals. Please be on your best behaviour as this client is important to my business. We need to impress him, okay?"

Avery nodded. "Sure. I can do that."

Ethan's brows snapped together. "Yes, you can."

A look of annoyance crossed Ethan's face. He placed his cutlery down and glared at Avery. "I'll say it again. Yes, you can do that for me. It's not like you have anything else to do now, is it?" he snapped. His eyes fixed on Avery, awaiting her response.

She knew how to navigate his moods to avoid a beating and smiled. Something she'd mastered as a child, to avoid her mother's drunken wrath. "I'm sorry, of course. I am happy to do it. You will be proud of the feast I will cook for you."

Ethan's tone softened. "That's more like it. And be sure to wear the black dress I bought for you last month. I think your hair tied up would work well, too. Right then, I must go. I will be back later with my client. Have dinner ready for six o'clock sharp and to reiterate, wear my suggestion please, nothing revealing. I want you to look classy, not slutty. Oh, and please clean the house," he demanded, and then left swiftly.

Avery listened to Ethan's car pulling off the driveway and drew in a harsh breath. She placed her head in her hands and cried for the longest time. *How did I get here? How did I allow this to happen to me after everything I went through with my mother? I'd just bought my first home. I loved it. I was living my dream life. At least I still have my job, thanks to Jax. How could I have been so blind? The red flags were there all along. Willow tried to warn me, but I refused to listen. Love felt too good, something I had never felt before—but it was not real. Love is never real.*

After pulling herself from her thoughts, she cleared the plates, washed up, and cleaned the house, then headed upstairs for a quick shower. The landline ringing caught her attention. She wrapped herself in a towel and headed downstairs to answer the phone. "Hello?"

"Hi, can I speak to Ethan?"

"I'm sorry, he's at work right now. Can I take a message?"

"Sure. Can you tell him his brother called?"

"Oh, hi. I'm Avery."

"Avery, yes, Ethan mentioned you. Maybe one day we shall meet in person. You should both head to Australia sometime."

"Sounds lovely. Something to consider."

"Well, I hope to meet you one day soon, Avery. Tell Ethan to call me back when he gets a moment. Bye for now."

Surprised by the call, Avery placed the phone on the receiver and messaged Ethan. He read her message and left her on *read*. Avery knew when he did that, it never ended well for her. Nervous now, she rushed upstairs and found the plain black shift dress Ethan had mentioned earlier. She slipped it on, tied her hair loose at the nape and applied minimal makeup before heading downstairs to prepare a special dinner to impress Ethan's client. Flicking through her cookbook, her finger rested on the one-pot chicken chasseur with creamy mash and crusty bread. A French bistro classic that she knew Ethan loved. She gathered the ingredients, prepped the cooking pot, and began slicing and dicing. She popped on some music to ease her anxious mind, but the song evoked memories of the past and sent her back in time to her mother's house. The damp smell of the walls, the stench of alcohol and unmade, dirty beds flashed through her mind. An icy shiver travelled through her body as thoughts of her childhood took centre stage in her head. Recalling the fear that she experienced daily and the nightly strangers that took over the house made her weep for the little girl that she once was. Avery wished she could reach out to her and give that lonely, scared girl a much-needed hug, something she rarely experienced as a child. She snapped herself out of it and focused on the meal preparations. Swiped the tears from her cheek and pulled herself together as she always did.

Avery glanced at the clock and panicked. She checked the dining table over and over until it satisfied her everything was in place. The wine was cooling in the ice bucket. The best cutlery laid out and serviettes folded just how Ethan liked them to be.

The key turning in the front door startled Avery. She looked up at the clock on the wall. *He's early!* She dashed to the dining table and checked it over one last time. *That will have to do.* She spun around as Ethan and his guest entered the dining room. She forced a smile.

Ethan played the part of the perfect husband. He walked over and planted a kiss on her cheek. "This all looks lovely. I would like you to meet Daniel Moore."

Avery extended her hand. "Pleased to meet you and welcome to our home."

Daniel smiled. "The pleasure is all mine."

Avery averted his gaze. Ethan's eyes fixed firmly on Avery as she dashed to the kitchen.

"Your wife is beautiful. You're a lucky man, Ethan."

"I sure am. Take a seat. I will be back in a moment." Ethan headed straight to the kitchen. His face was like thunder. He grabbed Avery by the arm and pulled her to him. "Never embarrass me like that again. Do you understand?"

Avery flinched, surprised. "What did I do wrong?" she whispered.

"You know exactly what you were doing. Acting like a whore in front of me. You were flirting with him."

Avery took a step back from Ethan and retrieved her arm. "I promise you, I wasn't. I'm sorry. I don't know what you want me to say." She swallowed a lump in her throat and wiped her eyes, praying it would all end. But she had a few more days to suffer until she was free from Ethan.

Ethan regained his composure and stepped away from Avery.

"Bring the dinner through now. After a few minutes, say you have a headache and leave the table. Your job is done for the evening."

Ethan left Avery shaking in the kitchen. She held her stomach and fought back her tears, before pulling herself together and serving the meal.

Daniel noted Avery's red, watery eyes and commented. "Is everything okay? You don't look too well."

Avery shook her head. "I'm sorry. I have a migraine coming on. I'm afraid I need to lie down. Again, I'm sorry."

Daniel stood up like a gentleman when Avery did. "I hope you feel better soon, Avery. It was lovely to meet you. Thank you for dinner. It looks delicious."

Avery dared not look at Daniel. She turned and headed up the stairs, leaving Ethan to entertain his client.

"I'm sorry about that, Daniel," she heard him say.

"Avery suffers from the most debilitating migraines from time to time. They come on without warning. Now, back to business."

* * *

Several hours later, Ethan wrapped up business with Daniel.

"Thank you, Ethan. Please thank your lovely wife for dinner," said Daniel as he left.

"I will let Avery know."

Ethan closed the door and headed straight to the bedroom. Avery pretended to be sleeping, but that did not deter Ethan. He pulled the quilt from her and threw it on the floor. Avery sat up, startled.

"What's wrong?" she asked.

"You, that's what's wrong. I saw the way you looked at Daniel." Ethan grabbed her by the feet and yanked her across the bed. He pressed his face right into Avery's. "Now get undressed," he ordered.

Revulsion filled Avery's body. She tried to inch away from him to no avail. He pulled her close and ripped off her nightshirt. "Never disrespect me again. Now turn over. I don't want to look at your face."

Avery fought back the tears, knowing what was coming.

Her body trembling annoyed Ethan. "*I said turn over*," he yelled.

Avery slowly turned over. She felt the weight of Ethan's body behind her as he pulled her up on to her knees and entered her with such force she yelped. He pushed her face down into the mattress so she could barely breathe. Panicked, she fought to raise her head, but Ethan forced her head deeper into the mattress, leaving little space for her to breathe. Once he'd finished, he climbed off her, picked up the quilt from the floor, and threw it over her. "Now clean yourself up. You look a mess."

Ethan left the room and returned downstairs. Avery pulled the quilt around her and curled up into a ball, unable to fight the tsunami of tears that followed, choking on the lump at the back of her throat.

CHAPTER TWENTY-SIX

*J*ax sat at the back of the coffee shop in Westwick, as agreed with Avery. He checked his watch, noting that she was fifteen minutes late. He knew he could not call her, as Ethan checked her phone all the time and might be with her. The last thing he wanted to do was cause more problems for her. He waited another ten minutes, and was just about to leave when Avery rushed in.

She smiled at the sight of Jax, she headed straight to him.

Jax noted Avery's hollow cheeks. Her clothes hung off her and the dark circles under her eyes worried him. "Are you okay?" he asked.

She swept her hair off her face and nodded. "I will be. I'm so sorry that I'm late. Ethan just wouldn't leave. He took his time this morning. I had to be sure he would not come back before I left. He does this thing some mornings, where he leaves for work and then re-appears a few minutes later saying he forgot something. But I know he is just checking on me or trying to catch me out on something. He's getting suspicious, Jax. I can feel it."

"Hey, don't worry. There is no way Ethan can know. You're

scared and I get that. But trust me, he can't possibly suspect anything. Now listen, I don't have long. I need to get back to the office for an important sponsor meeting this morning. Your project details for Africa are all set. I have given them to Willow. She will meet you at the airport on Monday and give them to you, along with your passport. If I could be there myself, I would, but my wife has her first scan Monday morning and I must be there."

"Of course, you have to be there with her. This is your child, and nothing is more important than that. Hug Julia from me. I am truly happy for you both."

"I will. Julia has been worried about you, as we all have."

Avery placed her hand on Jax's arm. "Thank you for everything. You didn't have to go to these lengths for me. If Ethan finds my passport and documents missing, I don't know what he will do. I just need to make it through until Monday morning. Only two days left."

"Willow and I are with you all the way. If there is anything you need, just let us know. I know you can't call or message me. But find a way if things go south on Monday, okay?"

"I will. I promise. But nothing can go wrong. It's got to work out, Jax. I can't carry on like this. I need to get as far away from Ethan as possible. He has become more unpredictable of late..." Avery paused and turned away from Jax. She swiped a tear escaping down her cheek. "I'm afraid of what he will do to me."

Jax placed his finger under her chin and lifted it. "We got your back. The plan is good. You must make it through to Monday. Don't give Ethan any reason at all to be suspicious. I know his type, believe me. I was brought up by one just like him. My mother suffered for years at the hands of my father, but that's a story for another time."

It surprised Avery to learn about Jax's father. He had never discussed his private life before. "Thanks for sharing that with me. I'm sorry you and your mother suffered."

"I just wanted you to know I understand your situation, and it wasn't something I was saying to make you feel better," Jax confessed.

"Thank you. Well, one thing I know for sure is that Tanzania, will be perfect for me. I can't wait to see the team again. I've missed them so much."

"And they have missed you, too. Jenny has talked about nothing else. Each time we talk on the phone, she is all about you and how excited the team is about your arrival. I must go now. Be careful, Avery. And call me once you reach Tanzania. Willow will let me know as soon as you have boarded the plane on Monday." Jax hugged Avery and left.

Avery ordered a latte and sipped it slowly while the events of the last couple of days replayed in her mind. Only adrenaline had kept her going for the last week, now she was almost at the finish line. The thought of two more nights under the same roof as Ethan sent chills running down her spine. She shivered and gripped her warm mug with both hands. *You're almost there, Avery, and then you will be free again.*

Ethan sat hunkered down in the layby on the far side of the square, raging. He watched Jax leave the coffee shop and fought an urge to jump out of the car and punch him. "You are an interfering little prick," cursed Ethan. He refocused his attention on Avery, watching her sipping her coffee. "You think you are so clever, Avery Masters? I will show you otherwise, you deceitful bitch." Ethan slammed his hands down on the steering wheel in rage. Then he calmed himself, pulled out of the layby and sped off.

Avery finished her coffee, left the coffee shop, and headed back home before Ethan arrived home for lunch. As she approached the house, her mouth dropped open. Ethan's car was already on the drive. Her heart thumped through her chest. She drew in a hefty slow breath to calm herself. *Okay, where have I been? That's the first question he'll ask. I popped into town for some halibut. Yes, that will work. The fishmongers were all out today. I can say that. It's not a fish they always have a substantial supply of, and Ethan knows this.*

Avery climbed out of her car, locked it, and headed for the door. Before she could retrieve her key from her handbag, the door swung open. Ethan stood back, his face void of emotion, and beckoned her in.

"I thought I would come home a little earlier today. Can you imagine my surprise when I found you were not here?"

Avery shrank away from him and attempted to walk past, but Ethan gripped her arm tight. "I'm sure you have a reasonable explanation, though. So, let's hear it?" he demanded.

Avery struggled to get her words out.

"Well, it's not a hard question. Where were you?"

"I, I ugh, I popped into town to get some halibut for our lunch. But the fishmongers didn't have any today. I'm sorry. I will make something else instead."

Ethan loosened his grip and began pacing the floor. "Look at me, Avery."

Avery lifted her head and looked at Ethan.

Ethan continued. "So, you went into town?"

Avery nervously nodded. "Yes."

Ethan continued to pace the floor, and then his entire stance softened. He stopped in his tracks, turned to Avery, and smiled. "So, what are you going to make us for lunch instead?"

Confused by his sudden change in tone, Avery straightened up and smiled. "I am going to make a light pasta dish instead."

She turned on her heel and headed into the kitchen. Ethan remained where he was, not taking his eyes off her until she rounded the corner out of sight. He noted her bag on the floor and began rifling through it. His anger resurfaced when he found nothing but her purse and some old shopping receipts. He flipped open her purse and searched for her bank card, but it was not there. Just a crumpled twenty-pound note and some loose change.

"Where the hell is her bank card and her credit card, for that matter?" Ethan took off his jacket and headed upstairs to the spare bedroom. He retrieved his document box from behind the wardrobe. He sat on the bedroom floor rifling through it but couldn't find Avery's passport, birth certificate or any other of Avery's documents.

"What the actual fuck?" he said aloud. He shut the box and shoved it back into the wardrobe. *I don't know what the hell you think you're doing, Avery Masters. I will find out.* Ethan headed back downstairs to join Avery in the kitchen.

His forced smile was not lost on her. "Dinner's ready."

She plated up and laid the table. They both sat down and began eating. Ethan periodically glanced at Avery with a forced smile. "This is lovely. Can I have some more?"

Avery nodded, kicked her chair back and went to refill his plate. "Here you go. Glad you like it. There's plenty more."

"Thanks. What do you have planned for the rest of the day?" he asked.

"I'm not sure. I'm going to take a bath and take it from there," she responded while focusing her eyes on her pasta.

Ethan finished his lunch, drank down his wine, and left the table. "I need to get back to the office. Daniel is dropping by this afternoon. Hopefully, he has agreed to partner with me on my latest project. Let's hope for your sake that he has." Ethan grabbed his jacket and left the house. His last words left an uncomfortable taste in Avery's mouth.

Avery drew in a deep breath and slumped back into her chair, relieved to be alone at last. *My nerves are shot. I can't take much more of this. Monday cannot come around soon enough.*

Avery only had that afternoon alone to double-check her hidden packed bags. There would not be another chance over the weekend.

Ethan would return home at five as he did every Friday. There would not be another chance. The knot in her stomach increased and made her feel nauseous. The thought of Ethan stumbling on her plan or preventing her from leaving the house amped up her anxiety.

* * *

Ethan arrived home at exactly five pm in a bad mood. Avery plated up dinner as he walked in and slammed the front door behind him.

He burst into the kitchen. "Ask me how it went with Daniel today?"

Avery looked at him knowing it went badly and afraid to speak.

"Okay, I will tell you how it didn't go: it did not go my way, Avery. And why do you think that is?"

Avery stood in front of him nervously.

"Are you deaf?"

"I'm sorry."

"Sorry for what? I haven't told you what happened yet!"

Ethan inched closer to her. "But yes, sorry you should be. Daniel decided to go with another company. He felt they were a better fit."

Ethan paused and glared at Avery for the longest time. Avery shifted nervously on her feet.

"It's your fault. You are the reason I lost a client. You, alone. And do you know why?"

Avery shook her head. Fear coursed through her veins.

"Well, I will tell you. Your poor hosting skills made me look bad. You disappear off to bed feigning a migraine made me look bad. The whole God-damn mood of the house made me look bad."

"But you told me to go to bed. You told me to say I wasn't feeling well."

Ethan raged. "What did you say to me?"

Avery stepped back and flinched.

"I think you must have heard me wrong. That is not how I remember it."

Avery knew no matter what she said, it would be wrong. She tried to merge with the back wall and prepared herself.

Ethan flew into a violent rage, picked up the rolling pin off the countertop and pummelled her back with it. He screamed, "You think your back is scarred now"– he spun around when his mobile phone rang. He dropped the rolling pin and answered. Changing his tone.

"Bro, you caught me at an inconvenient time. I'll call you tomorrow." Ethan cut the call and slipped his phone in his pocket. He turned to Avery. "Get up off the floor. I'm hungry."

Shaking, Avery rose to her feet, wincing in pain, while holding her back. She plated up dinner, sat down and waited for Ethan to join her. Ethan entered the room, pulled out a chair and sat down. His entire mood had shifted. "This looks lovely. What are you waiting for? Eat already."

Avery moved her food around the plate with her fork. Once Ethan finished eating, she was quick to leave the table.

Ethan followed her. "Oh no you don't. The dishes can wait." Ethan grabbed her hand and led her up the stairs.

"Please Ethan, I'm not feeling good. I need to soak my back."

Ethan glanced over his shoulder and glared at her. "You can bathe afterwards."

CHAPTER TWENTY-SEVEN

*M*onday morning, Willow wasted no time in getting ready to meet Avery at the airport. Skipping breakfast, she checked her bag to ensure all of Avery's documents were in place, then slipped on her loafers. She hunched her handbag over her shoulder and left the house. She halted in front of her car. "What the fuck? No way. Please, not today!" She rushed back into the house. Lucy emerged from the bedroom and appeared at the top of the stairs, "What's wrong?"

Willow rolled her eyes and threw her bag down on the floor beside the console. "My tyre is flat. What are the chances?"

"But you only pumped them up on Friday. Let me look." Lucy headed down the stairs, slipped on her slippers, and hurried over to Avery's car. Willow followed swiftly behind.

"See, totally flat!" pointed Willow.

Lucy knelt and inched closer to take a more detailed look. "It's not a standard flat. There is a large nail poking through it."

"What the fuck!" cursed Willow while kneeling beside Lucy. "How did that happen?"

Lucy shook her head. "Any number of ways. You drove home last night. How was it then? Did you notice anything?"

"No. It was fine and not flat when I arrived home last night."

"Maybe it happened in the day. It could have become flat overnight. The nail is acting like a plug, so the air is escaping slowly. Either way, you need to call the RAC. They will come and fix it," advised Lucy, climbing to her feet and heading back into the house.

"But I need it now, Lucy. I must get to the airport to meet Avery. I have her work documents and passport."

Lucy fetched her car keys out of the bowl and threw them to Willow. "Here, take theses. And I want my car back in one piece. Give Avery a big hug for me."

"Thanks, Sis. I owe you one. See you later."

Willow took a left out of the driveway and headed for the M6 North, towards the National Exhibition Centre. Traffic was light, cutting ten minutes off the journey. Willow checked the time on her dashboard. "Avery should be there now."

Before long, she was parking up in the short-stay carpark and paying for parking on her phone. "Fifteen pounds! You got to be fucking kidding me! This is insane," she cursed. "One hour should do it," she said aloud, taking her parking ticket from the machine and making her way towards the entrance.

She dashed through the automatic doors and turned right towards Costa Coffee, as she had arranged with Avery. On arrival, she scanned the coffee shop, but Avery was nowhere to be seen. She checked her phone. "Come on, Avery. You should be here by now. Where the fuck are you?" Willow bought herself a coffee and sat down at the only table available, centred in the middle of the busy shop. She watched people come and go for over thirty minutes then left. She stood outside anxiously, looking around. *She must be almost here. I should be okay to call her now,* she mused. She swiped to call and selected Avery's number. The call went straight to voicemail. "Damn it," she blurted.

Avery. I hope you haven't changed your mind. Willow walked slowly

144

towards the check-in area and searched for her friend. No Avery. She checked her phone again; one hour had passed since she'd arrived. Willow headed towards the exit, shaking her head. Outside, Willow waited a few more minutes just in case Avery showed up. Finally, she gave up and headed to her car. She climbed in and called Jax before heading off.

"Willow. Did everything go according to plan?"

"Hell no. Avery was a no-show. I tried calling but was directed to voicemail. Do you think she changed her mind or got scared?"

"No, I don't. She was determined to get as far away from Ethan as soon as possible. There is no way she would have changed her mind. Something's gone wrong, I can feel it. Keep trying her number. If we haven't heard from her in a couple of hours, come pick me up and we will head over to her house together."

"Good idea. I will be in touch later. Thanks, Jax." Willow cut the call and pulled away, her anger at the price of parking forgotten.

CHAPTER TWENTY-EIGHT

(A few hours earlier)

*A*very's hands shook as she pulled down the ladder to the loft and climbed up. She switched on the light and reached for the small suitcase and hand luggage. She carefully heaved them down the ladder and pressed the button, so the automatic ladder folded back up and the entrance closed. Avery dragged them into her bedroom, opened them, and did one last, thorough check. She rifled through her drawers and closet and threw in a few more things before zipping up the suitcase, unaware that Ethan was watching her from the doorway. She hadn't heard him creep up the stairs. When she turned around, she yelped in shock, shrinking back towards the wall.

Ethan stepped into the room with a sinister smile on his face. "And where do you think you are going?"

Avery knew he had caught her. There wasn't an excuse in the world that could talk her out of this. "I'm leaving. I can't do this anymore—I can't do us."

Silence dropped a heavy atmosphere over them. Ethan casually strolled across the room and unzipped her suitcase, flinging it over. He then did the same with the holdall, emptying its contents.

"You are going nowhere today. Why do you look surprised? You think I didn't know what you were planning? I wasn't sure what exactly you were up to, but I had a pretty good idea you were up to something. So, I kept a closer eye on you. And a good job I did. I saw you with Jax in Westwick the other day. It didn't take long to put two and two together. I also saw you leaving Willow's house the other day. If you were expecting Willow to come pick you up today, I'm afraid she's been held up. Car trouble, I believe!"

Ethan paused and circled Avery.

"You have made a fool out of me for the last time. After everything that I have done for you. You fucking selfish bitch. You women are all the same."

Avery trembled in fear for what was to come. "I must go, Ethan. Please let me go," she pleaded.

Ethan inched closer. "I saved you. I loved you when no one else would. Not even your own mother loved you. But I did. And this is the thanks I get." He pulled his arm back, clenched his fist tight and smashed it onto her jaw. Avery let out a piercing scream. She felt her jaw crack beneath his fist and reached up to cradle it. But before her hand could reach her jaw, Ethan slammed another blow to her cheek, sending her toppling to the floor.

"Please, Ethan, stop."

Ethan ignored her, dragged her by her hair onto the bed, then climbed on top, towering over her and punched her ribs and stomach repeatedly. Avery screamed aloud until her voice was hoarse. "Ethan, stop. I beg you!"

"You will not leave me. I told you we would be together forever. There is only one way you are leaving this house, Avery..."

Avery cradled her stomach and ribs. She was sure he had cracked one or two of them. It hurt to breathe. She turned to him. And braved, "I don't love you anymore. So do your worst. I can't live like this."

"As you wish!"

Ethan backhanded her across the face, knocking her off the bed.

He wrapped her hair around his hand and dragged her out onto the landing at the top of the steep stairs. He dangled her body over the top of the steep staircase and then pulled her back repeatedly. "Do you get it now? There is only one way out for you, Avery. Your choice."

Avery tried to pull back, but the pain in her ribs was too much to handle. Ethan once again inched her closer to the top of the staircase, balancing her over the edge and pulling her back in again by her hair several times. Each time, Avery winced in pain as her torso stretched out, pulling at her painful ribcage.

"I repeat, there is only one way you are leaving this house without me. I don't think you have grasped the magnitude of your situation. Look where we are right now. You did this to us. You, Avery. No one else will ever love you. Look at you. You're a mess. You're damaged goods. Scared of your own shadow. You have too much baggage for the average man to deal with. But I gave you a chance. I loved you and took care of you and this is how you repay me. No wonder your mother turned to alcohol. Do you see now what you do to people." Ethan stopped dead mid-rant. He lost his footing and wobbled on the edge of the top step. While he tried to balance himself, Avery saw her chance and took it. Without thinking, she battled through her pain, reached out her left arm, and pushed it into his stomach with all the force she could muster. Ethan's grip on her hair loosened and his eyes widened. His gaze remained locked on Avery's face as he fell backwards down the steep staircase. It seemed to happen in slow motion. Avery could hear his head crash against each step to the bottom. Avery crumpled to the floor and lay her head down over the top step. Her eyes remained fixed on Ethan's face. His eyes were wide open and flickering. She observed the light in them go out until they were void of life. His contorted body lay perfectly still at the bottom of the stairs. Relief washed over her.

CHAPTER TWENTY-NINE

(Present day)

Furled in a foetal position, her cheeks drenched from tears, and fighting the urge to close her eyes, Avery dug in her jeans pocket for her mobile phone. Barely able to see through her swelling eyes while navigating the keypad. After several attempts, she tapped 999, wincing through each breath drawn. The pain in her ribs disabled her with each move. Avery placed her hand over her rib cage while endeavouring to stay awake.

"Emergency Which service do you require, fire, police, or ambulance?"

"Ambulance. Police," struggled Avery.

"And your name and telephone number?" requested the operator.

Avery faintly revealed her name and number to the operator.

"I am transferring your call to the force control room. Stay on the line, Avery."

Avery was losing her battle to remain conscious. She laid her head down on the floor.

"Hello Avery, my name is Sofie. Can you state your location for me?"

Silence ensued.

"Avery... are you there?"

Avery's eyes flickered open. The distant sound of a woman's voice echoed through her phone. "I'm here," she whispered.

"Good. You are doing great, Avery. Stay with me. Where are you located?"

"III Church Street, Finswick. I'm hurt. He's dead..." Avery trailed off. The overwhelming desire to sleep arrested her and unconsciousness prevailed.

"Avery, are you still with me?" pressed the operator.

No response.

"If you can hear me, Avery, we have pinpointed your location. Someone is on their way to you."

* * *

Willow pulled up outside Jax's house. She checked her messages.

"I'm two mins away. Wait there."

Willow fidgeted anxiously while looking out of the back window periodically until Jax's car came into view. She leapt from her car and ran over to Jax.

"Jax, are you ready to go?" pressed Willow, glancing over to the passenger side and noting a wide-eyed Julia.

"Hi Julia, I'm so sorry about this."

"Don't be. I totally understand.

Jax interrupted them. "I just need to grab something from the house."

Willow nodded and turned her attention back to Julia. "How did the scan go?"

A huge smiled raised on Julia's face. "Perfect. We can talk about that another time. You and Jax need to go."

Jax emerged from the house. "I'm ready."

Willow waved goodbye to Julia and hopped into her car, followed by Jax.

"I have this awful feeling, Jax. I've heard nothing from Avery. She has not picked up any of my messages."

"Same here. I tried calling her after Julia and I left the hospital, but it directed to voicemail."

"Ethan's house is not far, ten minutes at most. Traffic is light, thank God."

Willow sped off and took a sharp left onto the primary route directly to Ethan's house. As the house came into view, Willow and Jax stared ahead in disbelief and looked at each other with raised brows. Two ambulances and several police cars surrounded the driveway. They noted two paramedics emerging from the house carrying a stretcher. A sheet covered the body entirely. Willow gasped, parked up, and leapt from the car. Jax followed.

A policewoman halted them as they rushed up the driveway. "Sorry, this is a crime scene. No one in or out."

"My best friend lives here, Avery Masters. I need to see her," Willow begged. Willow spun around when she heard the ambulance door shut. She turned back to the policewoman. "Please, I need to know." At that moment, another two paramedics emerged from the house. Willow instantly recognised Avery's long hair hanging over the back of the stretcher. She let out a tremendous sigh of relief. Jax gripped her arm. "She's alive! Thank God," he blurted.

Willow broke down, scooted past the policewoman and ran up to the paramedics. "I'm her best friend and only family. Is she okay?"

The paramedic holding the back end of the stretcher glanced at Willow's concerned, tear-drenched face. "She's alive, but critical. You can follow us to the hospital."

Willow's head bobbed up and down frantically. "Yes. Thank you. I will."

The policewoman caught up with Willow. "I will need to take a statement from you. Can I have your full name, please?"

"My name is Willow Forbes, best friend and only family to

Avery Masters. You can have your statement. But not now. Sorry, I need to get to the hospital. Avery needs someone with her."

The policewoman paused and glanced over to Jax and back to Willow. "That's fine. But you will both need to drop by the station later to give your statement."

Willow and Jax hurried to the car and followed the ambulance.

At the hospital they watched the ambulance rush Avery to accident and emergency. Willow drove into onsite parking, then had to battle with the onsite parking machine. "Here, let me sort this out. You go on ahead," Jax offered.

"Thank you."

Willow sprinted to the A&E reception desk.

"Hi, paramedics rushed Avery Masters through on a stretcher. I am her next of kin, and only family. She doesn't have anyone else."

The receptionist offered a sympathetic smile, tapped on her keyboard, and looked up at Willow, pacing frantically in front of her. "They have taken her through for emergency surgery. Can I have your full name, please?"

"Willow Forbes."

"Your relationship with the patient?"

"Friend and family."

"And an address and telephone number, please?"

Willow provided all the details requested and waited for the receptionist's response while she tapped her details into the system.

"Okay. Yes, I see we list you as Avery Master's next of kin. That's all I need. You can see her once they have moved her to the recovery ward. You may wait some time, though. We have a cafeteria on the second floor. You need to go through those doors over there on your right. Head on down to the end of the corridor and take a left and then an immediate right. There is a small waiting room. You can wait there. I will let the consultant know you are there for Miss Masters."

"Thank you so much." Willow hurried through the doors, following the directions until she reached the small clinical waiting room. She glanced around, surprised it was empty. She reached into her pocket for her phone and messaged Jax to let him know where she was. Then sent an update to Lucy.

Five minutes later, Jax burst through the doors. "How is she?"

Shaking her head, Willow answered. "I have no idea. Avery is in surgery. It must be bad. I can't believe this is happening. I knew Ethan was a bad one, but I never imagined he would go this far."

Jax couldn't sit down. He paced the floor angrily. "How could he do this to her? Avery is the most innocent person I have ever met. She did not deserve this."

Willow stood up. "I know. But that was the problem. Avery is too innocent, and she never knew what genuine love looked like. She certainly never got it from her mother. Her tough childhood lacked any kind of love. Avery rarely talked about it. But from what I got, it was bad. When Ethan came along and loved-bombed her, he was luring her until he firmly caught her in his net. Avery did not see Ethan coming. And again, she had been physically and mentally abused by someone that she loved. I don't know if she will recover from this."

Jax took Willow's hand. "She will recover because she has us. And we will be there for her."

Willow slumped down on the chair and buried her head in her hands and cried. Jax sat beside her with a comforting arm over her shoulder. Eventually, he stood and went to the canteen to fetch them a coffee.

CHAPTER THIRTY

*I*t seemed like forever before the consultant arrived. A tall man, with a rough-looking beard that needed a good trim. He sat opposite Willow and Jax.

"Hi, my name is Doctor Choudhary, Avery's consultant. I'm sure you are eager to know how she is doing, so I will get straight to it. Avery is in a critical but stable condition. I have transferred her to the intensive care unit for the next 24 hours. She has suffered a hairline fracture to the jaw and two hairline fractures to her ribs. We have placed Avery on a breathing machine to aid her through these first few hours. Unfortunately, we discovered an internal bleed. This was our greatest concern. We located and stemmed the bleed. But we will need to keep a close eye overnight. Hopefully, all being well, I will have her transferred from the ICU tomorrow. But it all depends on how she fares during the night. The good news is the baby is fine. Quite the miracle, considering the horrendous beating she took."

Willow and Jax were speechless.

Willow piped up. "Baby?"

"Yes, Avery is in her first trimester. I gather you didn't know?"

Willow shook her head. "No. I didn't know."

The consultant continued. "Right. Well, I suggest you go home for a while. Avery won't be waking up for some time yet."

Willow jumped in. "No, I'm staying here. I don't want her waking up alone. She will need someone to be there, a friendly face. You understand."

The consultant rose to his feet. "That's fine. One of my nurses will let you know when you can see her. Once Avery's settled in the ICU, you can sit with her."

"Thank you," cried Willow.

Dr Chaudhary's beeper went off. He glanced at it and made his way to the door. "I have another emergency. Please excuse me."

Willow kept shaking her head in disbelief. "If all this isn't bad enough, she will wake up to find she is carrying Ethan's child. I can't process this, Jax. It's a nightmare."

"Look, why don't I take your car, drop by your house, and get you an overnight bag? Message your sister to organise it for you. I will grab you a sandwich, too. You will need to eat later, and the canteen closes for the day shortly."

Willow turned to him. "Thank you. I don't know how I would have coped without you today. That would be great. I shall message Lucy now."

"Willow, just so you know, Julia and I will be here should you need us."

"I know and thank you."

Jax left, and Willow began typing a brief message to Lucy. After she pressed send, she went to the canteen for another coffee before it closed.

CHAPTER THIRTY-ONE

*A*very's eyes flashed open. The swelling eclipsed her view. Her face contorted with each breath. She cradled her rib cage to alleviate the pain. The crackling of her ribs shook her.

"You're awake! Good, how are you feeling?" asked the nurse, standing at the foot of her bed with a clipboard in hand.

Avery didn't respond. Disoriented, her eyes frantically scoped the room until her eyes rested on the nurse's face. His warm smile focused on Avery.

The nurse noted her concern and attempted to ease her mind. "It's okay. You are in hospital. My name is Aiden. Take it easy and don't move too much."

Avery searched Aiden's face and her eyes shifted to his name tag, which confirmed what he said.

Aiden offered a warm smile. "You are safe now, Avery."

He hung the clipboard on the foot of the bed, reached for a glass of water off the table, and held the straw to her lips.

"The consultant will be along shortly to speak with you."

Avery's eyes trailed over the young nurse. His fair hair glistened in the sunlight peeking through the blinds. His face was kind and genuine.

"Your friend Willow stayed with you throughout the night. Once you were off the critical list, we encouraged her to go home, freshen up, and then come back. She sure is stubborn, though!"

Avery's lip curled.

"I will be back later to check on you," Aiden said as he left.

The realisation of what happened hit Avery like a brick, transporting her back to her bedroom. She could see the rage on Ethan's face as he pummelled her body with his enormous fists in a violent rage. Her jaw cracked beneath his force. Panic consumed her while trying to fight him off, but Ethan was too strong. All she could do was protect her face and body by curling up into a ball to lessen the impact of his brutal force. The pain was more excruciating with each blow. Avery thought he would never stop. She raised a hand to the back of her head and felt blood oozing. An image flashed before her of Ethan dragging her by the hair off the bed and onto the landing at the top of the staircase. Fear coursed through her like a surge of electricity at the realisation of Ethan's intentions. At that moment, it was her or him...

There was no escaping her last image: Ethan lying contorted and broken at the foot of the staircase. His eyes flickered while the remnants of life drained from his body. Avery focused on Ethan's eyes until they closed permanently. His body lay perfectly still. An image she would never forget. Relief gripped her, followed by intense guilt.

Avery didn't have to wait too long before her consultant entered the room. Her eyes shifted to the door as a tall, bearded man entered, sporting a bright smile.

"You're awake! Good," he said while pulling up a chair beside Avery's bed.

"My name is Dr Chaudhary. And how are you feeling today?"

"Sore. My jaw hurts and my ribs too."

"That's to be expected. The pain will ease over the coming days as you heal. In the meantime, I will prescribe medication to help you through it."

Avery nodded. "Thank you."

Dr Chaudhary flipped through his papers and then glanced up. "Avery, were you aware that you are pregnant?"

Avery gripped her bed sheet in shock, and she tensed up. Her eyes flashed wide. "No. I can't be."

"Yes. You are seven weeks pregnant. The baby is doing fine."

"But..." Avery's voice trailed off. Her mind flashed back to an image of her face down on the bed while Ethan forced himself on her—one of several times. Her heart sank, her eyes teared up, and she turned away from Dr Chaudhary.

"You don't have to think about that right now. Let's focus on getting you well and back home."

Dr Chaudhary explained Avery's injuries to her and then left to continue his rounds. Aiden came back to check on her a few minutes later.

"How's my favourite patient doing?"

Avery brushed the tears from her cheeks. "I've had better days."

"A sense of humour. I like that. I just wanted to let you know that your friend, Willow, just called in asking if you were awake. She is currently on her way to see you. You have a good friend in Willow."

"I do." Avery turned to look out the window.

Aiden sensed she was not in the mood to talk. "Would you like something to drink or eat?"

"Yes, a coffee, please."

Aiden smiled. "One coffee coming up. Milk and sugar?"

"Just milk, please. Thank you."

Aiden turned on his heel and left the room. Avery placed her hand gently over her jaw as her mind wandered frantically, trying to understand why the people she loved treated her so badly. Echoes of her past lingered in her mind. Ethan's verbal abuse took centre stage, beating her down with words that cut through her like glass. She could visualise herself balled up on the bed, silently praying for him to stop, just like she used to with her mother when she unleashed her bitter tongue in an alcohol-fuelled rage. She was that little girl again, afraid and lost.

CHAPTER THIRTY-TWO

$\mathcal{W}$illow burst through the door and dropped her bag on the floor. She rushed to Avery, bent down, and kissed her forehead. "I wish I could give you a big hug. But your ribs, well, you know."

Avery gripped Willow's hand and squeezed. "Thank you for not giving up on me."

"Hey, as if I would. You are my best friend. I will always have your back." Willow paused and glanced at Avery's stomach, not knowing how to address Avery's pregnancy, and it did not go unnoticed. Avery piped up. "You know, don't you?"

Willow nodded. "I don't know what to say. It was such a shock. Were you aware?"

"Nope. I can't process it right now. It's just too much to handle."

"I get that. I can't imagine how you feel about it with everything that has happened. But I want you to know that whatever you decide. I am right by your side. Now, have you eaten today?" asked Willow, changing the subject.

"No, I don't think I could eat a thing right now. I've had a coffee and wouldn't mind another."

Willow leapt from her chair. "Consider it done. I won't be long."

Avery placed her hand over her stomach. *I don't think I can do this.* Her mind drifted back to her childhood. The dirty house, her mother's unpredictable nature and the drunk men that came through nightly like a passing train. She could almost hear her mother screaming at her, "You ruined my life, just like your father did. Don't think that you are any better than me. You will never amount to anything. Just look at you. Now get to your room. Before I do something I will regret."

Don't do this, Avery. Fight through this. Don't sink into the abyss or you will lose yourself.

Willow entered the room, juggling two coffees. "Here you go," she said, gently placing the coffee cup in Avery's hand. "Careful."

"I need a straw. The nurse left a bunch on the side table."

"Sorry. I didn't think." Willow reached for a straw and popped it into the cup.

"Have they said how long you will stay in here?"

"Not yet."

Willow talked for a minute before noticing that Avery had completely zoned out. Her eyes glazed as she focused on the swirling coffee. "Avery?"

"I'm sorry. What did you say?"

"I said Jax wants to drop by later if you're up to it?"

Avery nodded and drifted off again.

Willow placed her cup down and inched her chair closer. "Are you really okay? I'm worried about you."

"Not really. None of this feels real, Willow. I can't process anything. My mind is spinning. I want to wake up from this nightmare."

"I know." Willow gave Avery's hand a gentle squeeze. "You're not alone. I'm with you every step of the way."

Willow stood up. "I need to get off. But I will be back later this evening around seven. Do you need anything?"

Avery shook her head. "I don't think so. Thanks for everything. I'm lucky to have you. Just know I appreciate you."

Willow teared up, leaned forward, and kissed Avery on the cheek. "I love you and will always be here for you."

Avery grabbed Willow's hand and held it briefly. "Love you."

Willow's smile reached her eyes. "Love you too."

* * *

When Willow arrived home, Lucy was in the kitchen making brunch. "How's Avery?"

"She looks like a truck hit her. Avery's awake and processing the fact that she's pregnant and said little, only that she can't process the news right now. Defeated doesn't cover how she looks. I'm worried about her."

"Oh, my God! I can't imagine being in her shoes. After everything that she's been through because of Ethan and now she is pregnant. Shit, I can barely process it. I don't know how Avery will. Look, all we can do is to be there for her. She is going to need us all more than ever. She has a long road of recovery ahead and not just physical."

"I agree. Avery needs to know she is not alone. Because the look in her eyes today told me otherwise. It's as if she is mentally shutting down. As far as the baby is concerned, I don't know what she is going to do at this point. I let her know that whatever her decision is that we would all be there for her."

Lucy nodded. "Absolutely, one hundred per cent."

Willow spun around when Jackson entered the kitchen. "Hey, when did you arrive?"

Jackson went to the kitchen island and swiped a piece of toast off the plate. "About an hour ago. I want to visit Avery. She was there for me during my darkest time, and I want her to know I will be there during hers."

Willow smiled and darted a glance at Lucy.

"Avery will appreciate that. I think she needs to know she has the full support of us all."

"I am heading back this evening. So, why don't we stagger the visits rather than turning up en masse? You could drop by this afternoon's visiting slot."

"Sounds good to me. I will head over there after I have eaten." Lucy pushed a plate towards him. "Looks good, Sis!"

"Willow, do you want some brunch?"

"Yes, just a small plate for me. I need to go wash my hands."

Lucy turned to Jackson. "This has hit Willow hard. She loves Avery like a sister. You know how Willow is. She hides her emotions well and always has to be the strong one for everyone else. Let's monitor her, too. She almost lost her best friend, and I sense she is feeling vulnerable."

"Agreed. Now, you said you had something to tell me about Avery. What is it?"

"Avery is pregnant! She had no idea until this morning when her consultant informed her. Can you imagine that?"

Jackson's mouth dropped open. He fell silent while processing the news. He placed his knife and fork down and stood up. "No way. How has she taken the news?"

"She won't talk about it right now. I think she's struggling to process it all. She's in hospital with a fractured jaw, fractured ribs, and an internal bleed. Ethan is dead and if that is not bad enough, she is told that she is pregnant by her dead boyfriend..."

Jackson could not find the words to respond. "I'm sorry, Lucy, I can't finish this. I'm going to head over to the hospital."

Surprised, Lucy retrieved Jackson's plate and placed it in the dishwasher. "Ok, give Avery a hug for me and let her know I will visit tomorrow."

"Sure. Will do."

Jackson grabbed his coat off the back of the stool and left. Willow ambled into the kitchen and searched the room. "Where's Jackson?"

"He left for the hospital. I just told him Avery's pregnant!"

"Oh, right? Yep, that would have triggered him. Maybe she will open up to him as she did before. He seems to have a way with her that no one else does."

"Let's hope so."

CHAPTER THIRTY-THREE

*J*ackson paused in the doorway, inhaled a slow deep breath, and entered Avery's room with a fixed smile. His eyes rested on her sleeping face. The bruises and swelling shocked him. He pulled up a chair quietly, not wanting to disturb her. She looked tiny and fragile lying there, screaming vulnerability. He took her hand and closed his hand around it.

"You're not alone. We are all here for you. Willow, Lucy, Jax and me. We're here for you," he whispered.

Avery's eyes flickered open. Her lips curled. "Hey."

"Hey, how're you feeling?"

Avery eased herself into a more comfortable position. Jackson leant over to plump the pillow for her.

"I feel as if a truck hit me. It could have been worse, I guess."

Jackson placed his hand over hers. "Just know that I am only a phone call away. I'm here for you, no matter what. You will face nothing alone."

Avery's eyes welled up. Her lips quivered, and she tried hard not to cry.

Jackson inched forward. "Hey, it's okay to cry. Just let it out."

Avery allowed her tears to fall. She turned away from Jackson. He squeezed her hand. "You are so brave, Avery. You are the bravest person I know."

She slowly turned around to face him. "I don't feel brave. Scared, yes. I'm so scared. I don't know what I'm going to do. I'm pregnant, Jackson. What the hell am I supposed to do about that?"

"Right now, absolutely nothing. Just focus on getting better and out of here. Willow has made up the spare bedroom for you. Once you're discharged, you are staying with my sisters until you're back on your feet. So, there is nothing to worry about. As far as the baby is concerned, you have time and choices. You do what is best for you."

"That's the thing, Jackson. I don't know what I want. When I first heard about it I thought I did. But now, I'm not sure. I am struggling to get through today. I'm overwhelmed and the detective is coming later. I don't know what to tell them, Jackson."

"Just tell them what happened. That's all you can do."

"But that's the thing, I'm not sure. I keep going over it in my head. At the bottom of the stairs, I see a broken and still Ethan. He fell as if in slow motion. I watched from the top of the stairs as he took his last breath. I felt relieved, followed by intense guilt. But my first emotion was relief! What does that make me?" she cried.

"It makes you human. After everything that monster did to you, your response was human. You mentioned you felt intense guilt, right?"

Avery offered a weak nod. "Only a loving, decent human being would wrangle with feelings of guilt, Avery. That is who you are. So, what, you had a moment of relief. That is simple to explain: you were alive. You escaped death at Ethan's hands. That is the truth of it."

Jackson leant forward and wiped the tears tumbling down Avery's cheeks. "And that's what you tell the detective. You fought for your life. That is the truth. A moment of relief is not a crime. Okay?"

Avery placed her hand over Jacksons. "Thank you. I needed to hear that."

"Hey, like I said. I'm here for you, always. And if you need any advice on your secondary concern, just call on me. I won't pretend its easy being a single parent. It's hard as hell. However, the rewards outweigh all the stress. But I fully understand that your situation is completely different. I can't imagine being in your shoes right now. But like I said, bravest person I know!" he winked.

"It feels like a nightmare that I can't wake up from."

Jackson inched closer. "You will wake up from all of this, I promise you. One day, you will open your eyes, and this will be a section of your life that you can file. You will never forget it, but it will be a distant memory of another time in your life when you survived. You will emerge stronger for it."

Avery studied Jackson's face for the longest time. Gratitude welled up inside of her. "When did you get so wise?" she squeezed his hand, and he placed his on top of hers.

"Losing my wife and becoming a single dad aided in that department. My struggles taught me a few things. The least I can do is share them with you."

The nurse entering silenced them. Jackson stood up. "I'm going to pop into the canteen and give you some privacy. Do you want anything?"

Avery shook her head. "No, thanks."

She turned her attention to Aiden, who was his usual bubbly self.

"How are you feeling?" he asked.

"Sore. My jaw aches like hell."

Aiden reached for a small plastic pill pot off the trolly. "Well then, it's a good job I'm here. Time for your meds. Now take these." He handed her the pot and a beaker of water. "They will take the edge off for a few hours. Dr Choudhary advised two every three to four hours. They will help with the pain.

"Now, are you going to tell me who the ridiculously handsome man is?" he laughed, attempting to cheer her up.

Avery's eyes widened in surprise. "You mean Jackson? He's one of my closest friends."

Aiden turned when Jackson entered the room and offered Avery a cheeky smile, then left them to it.

"Everything okay?"

"Yep. It was time for my painkillers. I couldn't get through the day without them."

"What are those?" asked Avery.

"These are a sorry-looking bunch of flowers I just rescued from the poorly stocked hospital shop." Avery watched while Jackson arranged them in a vase on the window ledge.

"Thank you. You didn't have to do that."

"Yes, I did. The poor flowers had no hope otherwise," he winked.

"Jackson, will you come back tomorrow?"

He walked over, leant forward, and placed a kiss on her forehead. "Try keeping me away. I need to head off now, but Willow is dropping by this evening. Try to sleep for a while."

Avery watched Jackson until he disappeared out the door. Alone with her thoughts, she placed her hand over her tummy and rubbed it softly. A tear escaped from her eye. *What am I supposed to do?*

CHAPTER THIRTY-FOUR

*B*y day four, Dr Choudhary gave the all-clear for Avery to be discharged, with a list of strict instructions to follow and an outpatient visit for the following week. Jackson stuck his head through the door and smiled. "You ready?"

"So ready!"

Jackson smiled at Aiden.

Avery glanced at the wheelchair. "I won't be needing that, Aiden. I can manage."

"Are you sure?" Aiden asked.

"I'm sure. Thank you for everything."

Aiden smiled. "It was my pleasure. Take care of yourself."

Jackson picked up her bag, and Avery climbed to her feet slowly while looping Jackson's arm.

"Slow and steady," Jackson reminded.

"Trust me, there's no other speed for me right now."

Jackson chuckled, and they headed to the exit.

Jackson held onto Avery's arm as they exited the hospital and found their way to his car.

"Okay, let me open the door. Just place your hand on the car for support."

Jackson opened the car door, adjusted the passenger seat to give Avery more leg room, and then helped her into the car and belted her in.

"How's that?" he checked.

"Perfect. Thank you."

Jackson skipped around to the driver's side and hopped in the car. Avery cast her eyes over him as he strapped himself in, turned on the radio, and pulled out of the car park. A warm smile enveloped her face. Jackson turned to face her. "You okay?"

"I'm okay."

"Good. Let's get you out of here. Willow is desperate to have you home. So beware, she is in full nurse mode just for you and Ruby is busy drawing you a welcome home picture!"

CHAPTER THIRTY-FIVE

*W*illow flung open the front door when she heard Jackson's car pull up in the driveway. She rushed out the door to Avery. Jackson reached across Avery to unclip her seatbelt. Avery leant back to enable him to reach the clip. He turned to face her, his nose almost touching hers. "I'm sorry, the belt is a little stubborn."

Avery smiled. "It's fine, really."

Avery realised at that moment just how much Jackson had always been there for her. All these years he'd looked out for her. She recalled the time when he helped her to move into her rental apartment, carrying all the boxes, fixing the plumbing, and installing her washing machine while she stood back and drank wine with Willow. And how he fended off a persistent guy at the local pub who would not take no for an answer.

Before stepping out of the car, she placed her hand over his. "Thank you for always being there for me. You are a rock in my life, Jackson." She attempted to struggle out of the car.

"Wait, I got you." Jackson leapt out of the car and ran around to the passenger side. Willow watched as Jackson carefully aided Avery out of the car. She dashed over and intervened.

"Here, take my arm. I got her Jackson. Can you get her bag?"

"Sure."

* * *

Jackson paused and watched Willow and Avery slowly walk to the front door. He couldn't get over how fragile she was. His heart ached for the pain she had suffered in her life. He fetched Avery's bag from the boot, locked up his car, and headed into the house.

Ruby came rushing over to him. "Daddy!"

He dropped the bag and swept Ruby up in his arms. "Hey, beautiful. Have you been good for your aunts?"

Ruby nodded, giggled excitedly, and wriggled free from his arms. "Where are you going?" Ruby giggled her way into the living room.

Jackson followed swiftly behind. "Oh wow! The room looks great. So many balloons!" He shot a glance at Avery, who was quiet and looked overwhelmed. Tears filled her eyes. Jackson shifted his eyes at Willow. He locked eyes with her and darted his eyes to Avery. Willow understood and inched closer to Avery, placing her arm over her shoulder. "Come on, let me show you to your room."

"Thanks, Willow. You didn't need to go to all this trouble."

"Trouble! Hey, it was nothing. A few balloons, a dodgy homemade cake, and a few flowers. I did it for me really," she winked.

Avery attempted to smile and winced, remembering her fractured jaw.

"Oh God, I'm sorry. Note to self, don't make Avery laugh."

Once Willow and Avery left the room, Jackson slumped down on the sofa. Lucy came over to him. "Hey, you okay?"

"Just worried about Avery."

"I know you are. We all are. Did you get anything out of Avery about the baby and what she wants to do?"

"Not much. She can barely process the fact she's pregnant, let alone decide on it. I am worried she cannot handle it. Can you imagine the position she's in? I wish I could help her more. She is extremely vulnerable right now."

"I hear you. All we can do is to be there for her and help her through the next few weeks. Anyway, you are helping her, Jackson. You've been amazing with Avery. The two of you always had a deep bond. You have a way of getting through to her. Maybe you could offer her advice and share some of your experiences as a single father. Or even better, maybe it would be a good idea for Avery to spend time with you and Ruby. Stay with you both when she is more mobile. It will give her an informed view of parenthood and may make it easier for her to decide what she wants to do."

Jackson's eyes lit up. "Lucy, that's a genius idea."

"I do have them occasionally! I will mention it to Willow and see what she thinks and if she is on board with the idea, then maybe in a few weeks, once Avery is feeling stronger. She can spend a week with you and Ruby. The break from this town might be a good thing for her, too."

"Yep, I agree. Now what's for lunch? I'm hungry."

"I made creamy mushroom pasta."

"Perfect. A large bowl for me. Is there any garlic bread?"

"Of course! You can't have creamy pasta without garlic bread in this house."

Willow walked into the kitchen after helping Avery settle into her room. "She's having a sleep. I'm worried, Lucy. She barely said a word. She looks defeated to me."

"Jackson and I were just talking about Avery. I thought it might be a good idea when she's feeling a little better to spend time with Jackson and Ruby. Get out of this town for a while. But the main reason was to give her an insight into life as a single parent, should she decide to keep her baby."

"Wow, Lucy, I'm impressed!"

"Oh my God, not you as well. I do have some good ideas, you know."

Willow laughed, grabbed a slice of garlic bread off the plate, and dipped it into the large pasta dish cooling down on the countertop. "Mmm, this is good. Is it ready?"

"Yep, go tell Jackson I am plating up and can you take the cutlery through with you? Thanks."

Once they were all seated around the table, Jackson piped up. "So, we are all agreed on Lucy's idea?"

They all nodded.

Willow spoke first. "It's a great idea. And one I think Avery needs, too, even if she won't realise it at first. You have such a lovely big house and garden, Jackson. The way the garden backs onto a large meadow and all that space, it's just what Avery needs. It will give her time to think, too. I know she will be in excellent hands with you."

"That's what I thought, too," piped Lucy.

Jackson smiled, wiped the pasta sauce dripping from Ruby's mouth, and placed his fork down. "That's settled then. Let's hope Avery agrees."

Willow interrupted. "I will talk to her when the time is right and put it in such a way, she won't be able to refuse."

Lucy nearly spat out her pasta. "Now that I believe. You could convince anyone of anything."

"Oh, shut up!" Willow threw a crust at Lucy, just missing her head.

Jackson smiled widely. "I've missed this. It reminds me of the old days. You two teasing each other, mum and dad jumping in to break you both up before a full-on food fight occurred."

"Those were the days," chimed Lucy.

"You know, Avery never had what we had: a family that loved her, siblings to grow up with, longstanding friendships and parental security. I know she's been through hell. Thank God, she found us," said, Willow.

"Yep. But you know, your friendship with Avery brought the

best out of you, Willow. I think you needed Avery as much as she needed you," explained Jackson.

"All I know is that Avery is my soul sister. She's more than a best friend. She was always there to pick up the pieces after every breakup, every heartbreak, and every poor decision I made. She made everything better. And now, I want to make everything better for her."

Jackson reached over and squeezed Willow's shoulder. "And you will."

Lucy leapt from her chair. "Right then, I have things to do, and people to see. I will leave you two with the washing up! See you later."

Willow cast a glance Jackson's way, "Come on, let's get this over with."

CHAPTER THIRTY-SIX

*O*ver the weeks, Avery's physical injuries healed well, but her mental health remained fragile. Her pregnancy began to show. The more she showed, the more she retreated into herself, barely leaving her bedroom. Instead, Avery lay on the window seat and pulled the blanket over her while staring out of the window into the garden. As she placed her hand over her tummy and fought the urge to cry, she heard a faint knock on the door.

"Come in?"

Willow pushed open the door and entered. "Hey, how are you feeling this morning? I brought you breakfast."

"Thank you. I'm not feeling hungry, though."

"Well, you must eat something, Avery. You've barely been eating enough for a bird these past few weeks. You need your strength."

Willow placed the tray on Avery's lap. "Come on, just eat a little for me?"

Avery glanced over her plate and picked up a slice of toast.

"That's my girl," encouraged Willow.

Willow paced the floor trying to find the right words. She

stopped mid-track, turned, and knelt on the floor beside Avery. "There's something I've been meaning to talk to you about."

Avery searched Willow's face. "Okay."

"Well, we thought, by we I mean Jackson, Lucy, and me. We thought you could do with a break from this town. Somewhere to gather your thoughts. And what with your struggle due to your impending decision..." Willow paused and looked at Avery's belly. Avery turned away to face the window. Willow placed her hand on top of Avery's.

"We thought it would be a good idea for you to spend some time with Jackson and Ruby. A week maybe. You recall how amazing his house is, right?"

Avery turned around and nodded.

Willow continued. "And all that land he has that backs out onto the gorgeous meadow. Great for long, quiet walks. What do you think?"

Avery eased herself off the window seat and sat on the bed. Then glanced over to Willow, who was still kneeling on the floor. "Yes, I think you're right. It's just what I need. And Jackson agrees?"

"Of course he does."

"Then I would love to go. I think you're right. It's just what I need right now."

Avery's eyes darted down to her tiny bump. "I'm aware I need to decide soon. It's just so hard. I have barely processed this. I could not think about it. It's too hard. But I know I need to, and soon."

"This is great. And you know Jackson will take care of you. Ruby will love having you around, too. She's a fireball, that one! I wanted to ask you something else. I know you chose not to go to Ethan's funeral, and I get that. In your shoes, I wouldn't have gone either. But I was wondering if you'd thought any more about meeting his brother. He has called several times, wanting to see you. I think he feels responsible somehow."

Avery shook her head. "No, definitely not. Not yet anyway, if ever. Have you met him?"

Willow climbed to her feet. "Of course not. I would never meet up with him and certainly not without your knowledge. It's not my place. I was just curious how you felt about it, that's all. And there's the fact he went to a great deal of effort to find you."

Avery climbed off the bed and reached for her wash bag. "Truth is, Willow, I'm afraid to meet with him. I have no idea what he looks like. I know nothing about him. What if he looks like his brother? I don't know what to say to him. Do you think I need to meet with him? I'm thinking not."

"I get it. I will let him know if he calls again. You just need to concentrate on your mental health right now. Changing subjects, I cannot wait to tell Jackson that you have agreed to stay with him. He will be so happy. He's been incredibly concerned about you. I think he just wants to be there for you actively, as you were for him in the past."

"When was Jackson thinking of having me?"

"Whenever you're ready."

"Okay, well, it's Wednesday today, so would Friday be too soon? I think the change of scenery will be good for me."

Willow inched forward and enveloped Avery in a hug. "Leave it with me. I will call Jackson and sort it out."

"Okay. Thank you. I'm going to take a shower."

"Do you need anything?"

"No. I can manage. Thanks, Willow."

CHAPTER THIRTY-SEVEN

*J*ackson hauled Avery's bags into the boot of his car. Avery stood on the porch hugging Willow, whose eyes dripped with tears. Lucy jumped in and wrapped her arms around the pair of them. "Group hug."

Jackson stood back and smiled while shaking his head. "Anyone would think she was leaving the country! Let the girl go. She will be back soon enough."

Willow stepped back. "If you need anything, a chat or something, then call me."

Avery squeezed her hand tight. "I will. Thanks, Willow. I'm so lucky to have you."

Willow swiped the tear from her cheeks. "Go on before I jump in that car with you!"

Avery climbed into the back with Ruby and waved as Jackson pulled off the driveway and headed for the motorway. Ruby tugged on Avery's arm. Avery turned from the window, smiling at Ruby. She reached for Ruby's hand instinctively and held it. Ruby chuckled and closed her eyes, gripping Avery's hand. Jackson watched the exchange between them in his rearview mirror, and his heart melted. His smile reached up to his eyes while he drove. He popped on some music and drove steadily towards home. Every once in and while, he would glance over his shoulder to check on both the girls, who were now in a deep sleep and still holding hands.

* * *

Jackson drove down the long narrow, wooded lane until he reached his gates. He wound down his window, tapped in the code and waited for the gates to open. Avery stirred in the backseat. She half-opened her eyes and shot a glance out of the window. She turned back and observed Ruby, who was stirring. "We are home, Ruby."

Ruby yawned while Avery unclipped her car seat and heaved her out of it. "Come here." Ruby opened her arms and latched on to Avery. Jackson parked the car and opened the passenger door. "Here, let me take Ruby off your hands. You still need to be careful."

Avery climbed out and stood back, admiring the house and surrounding gardens.

"I forgot how beautiful and peaceful this place is. You've had the landscape gardeners in, I see. Looks amazing."

"Yeh, they have done an amazing job. Just wait until you see the back garden. Come on. Let's go inside."

Jackson carried the bags, Ruby held Avery's hand to the door. As soon as it opened, she let go of Avery's hand and made a beeline for Comet, their dark brown Siberian cat.

"Oh my God, you never mentioned you had a cat?"

"Yes, the latest addition to my family. The next-door neighbour has been feeding him while I've been away. She's good like that."

Avery knelt and stroked Comet, who was more than happy to receive the fuss.

"He's hypoallergenic, or as much as any cat can be, and he's tactile, so beware," Jackson informed.

"I don't mind at all. Way back, just after I bought my house, I was thinking of getting a pet. I never had one as a kid and always wanted one."

Avery shifted focus. "Bathroom still in the same place?"

"Yes, up the stairs and third door on your left. I will make us some coffee."

Avery glared at her reflection in the mirror. Her hollow eyes, dark circles, and patchy skin grabbed her attention. Shaking her head, she turned away from the mirror and returned downstairs. Jackson was in the kitchen feeding Ruby, and the smell of fresh coffee teased her senses. Avery pulled out a stool at the kitchen island and watched Jackson in awe.

"You are so good with Ruby. How do you do it?"

"I kind of grew into the role, to be honest. Before my wife passed, she did all this. Feeding Ruby and taking care of her while I was at work. I got the simple end of the deal back then. When I'd come home, my wife had fed and bathed Ruby," Jackson paused.

Avery piped up. "Well, you grew into the role fast and you're doing a wonderful job. Ruby is thriving."

"Yes, but it's hard at times. I cannot lie. When she was teething, I barely slept for months. Then came colic. That was a nightmare. I cried myself to sleep some nights during the early days. I missed my wife and found the transition to single parenthood hard. But I had to push those thoughts aside for Ruby. She needed me, she needed her father."

Avery's eyes darted to Ruby. Her big eyes and long lashes stared back at her. "And you wouldn't trade it all in for the world, right?"

Jackson smiled. "Absolutely right. Ruby is my life. She has kept me going all this time. I cannot imagine my life without her."

Ruby yawned. Jackson picked her up. "I need to put her down for a nap. She didn't nap for long on the journey here. I'll be back shortly."

"Sure, go ahead."

Avery stepped off the stool and headed for the sliding doors leading to the back garden. She pulled them open and gasped. The weeping willow tree in the centre of the never-ending garden was huge. The willow branches hung over the centre garden like a dome. "Wow!" she said aloud while walking around the garden. At the far end, there was a beautiful wooden pergola adorned with lights and climbers. The seating area surrounded a large stone fire pit and looked like something out of a House and Home magazine. Avery continued past the pergola until she reached the end of the garden and the beginning of the meadow. She inhaled a deep breath, taking in the fresh air. When someone tapped her shoulder, Avery screamed and almost fell back, but Jackson caught her mid-fall.

"Avery, it's okay. You're safe here." He enveloped her in a hug and felt her body trembling in his arms.

"I'm so sorry for everything you have suffered in your life."

Avery did not respond. She slowly pulled away from Jackson. "For a moment there..." she paused mid-sentence.

Jackson added. "I know. No explanation necessary."

Jackson felt the weight of Avery's trauma response. At that moment, he realised just how fragile Avery was. He vowed to himself to do everything he could to help her on her healing journey.

"Let's go back to the house, grab our coffees, and sit down for a while."

Avery walked alongside Jackson to the house. He poured two cups of coffee and pointed to the far window. "Over there. It's one of my favourite spots to drink my coffee while Ruby sleeps."

Avery sat down opposite Jackson and studied him intently. For the first time in her life, she saw him. His kindness and strength. His beautiful, chiselled face and intense dark blue eyes. Jackson caught her and locked eyes briefly. Jackson's heart raced, and he broke eye contact and stood up.

"Avery, can I ask you a question?"

Avery nodded. "Sure, but I can't guarantee an answer."

"What happened to you as a child? You never really spoke about it to any of us. You shared a little here and there, but you hide so much pain. I know it was bad and the memory of it is painful. I just had to ask."

Avery's face paled. She turned and faced the garden.

"Forget I asked. It was insensitive of me. It's too much for you to share right now."

Avery remained silent for a while longer, contemplating her words, and then turned to face Jackson. "You really want to know?"

"Yes, I really do. But only if you're ready."

Avery took a deep breath. She clasped her hands together tight. Jackson observed her intently.

"My childhood was my hell on earth. The whole time I lived in fear, crouching in dark corners so as not to be noticed. Afraid of shadows lurking in corners. I spent hours upon hours locked in my bedroom when my mother entertained strays she'd brought back from the pub. They were all so drunk and loud. I watched my bedroom door handle move up and down many times and feared that one day, one of those drunks would get in." Avery took a beat. Jackson did not say a word.

Avery continued. "On scorching summer nights, it was unbearable, because my mother nailed shut the windows in my room. The heat was too much to bear. Mother unlocked my door in the mornings before I woke. I would find her on the couch with vodka and beer bottles strewn across the floor. The potent smell of stale cigarette smoke permeated the air. I had to navigate all that daily while getting myself ready for school. No breakfast, no clean clothes, just navigating the gauntlet until I made it out of the house."

Jackson placed a hand over Avery's arm and squeezed it. "God, Avery, I can't imagine having to suffer that. I'm so sorry you had to go through that." He swiped a tear trailing down his cheek.

"The thing is Jackson, that wasn't even the worst of it. Over time, the neighbours began calling social services to alert them to my mother's neglect of me. In the end, they removed me from my mother's care. I can recall walking through the living room, bewildered and scared. My mother passed out on the couch as I left. Not a sound from her. No fight to keep me. No goodbye—nothing."

Jackson's eyes welled up. "You deserve so much more than the hand you were dealt. Just know that you have a family now. Willow, Lucy, Ruby, and me. We are your family now."

Avery's lips curled. "I know that." After a brief pause, Avery continued.

"Once they placed me in care, things went from bad to worse." Avery stopped talking. She choked back a lump in her throat and paced the floor. Jackson noted her anxiety and stepped in.

"You don't have to say anymore if it's too painful."

"No. I want to tell you. I need to tell you. While in the children's home, I was raped and beaten several times over several months by the night security guard. I fought hard too, but it made things much worse. I tried to run away, but he caught me and beat me into submission. He put the fear of death into me and said if I told anyone, I would not live to see another day. After some time, it stopped. He moved on to the next girl and then the next girl. I soon discovered that there were several members of staff doing the same thing. Many years later, a whistle-blower who was an ex-member of staff, one of the good ones, brought to light what had been going on there and the guilty ones were brought to justice after a huge investigation. That is my full story. Well, almost." Avery stood in front of Jackson, turned her back to him and undid her shirt.

He stood up. "Avery, what are you doing?"

She ignored him and took off her shirt, baring her back.

Jackson gasped in horror and stepped back. Tears filled his eyes. "Oh my God, no! Damn them." He suppressed the rage inside of him. He wanted to scream, but on the surface remained calm.

Avery remained with her back to Jackson. Revealing her truth opened up all of her emotions, her tears cascaded and her body trembled. Jackson picked up her shirt and wrapped it around her shoulders. He enveloped her tightly, pulling her close to him.

"No one will hurt you again. Never. You are not alone anymore, Avery. You have a family now. Do you hear me?"

Avery burst into uncontrollable tears. She cried so loud and hard that Jackson could hear her inner pain reaching out. He could hardly bear it. He held her tight until she was all cried out. Eventually, she wiped her face and released herself from Jackson's embrace.

"I'm so sorry. That was too much for us both. Maybe a hot bath would be good for me right now."

"Hey, look at me." Jackson placed both of his hands on her cheeks. "Never be sorry for your truth. Now, I will get the bath ready for you. Come on, I will show you to your room."

Avery followed behind Jackson to her room. Jackson flung open the bedroom door. Avery's eyes widened. "Oh Jackson, this is beautiful. Thank you."

"I have one more cool surprise for you." He opened the door at the far end of the room. "Come here," he beckoned.

Avery walked over and peeked through the door. "Oh, Jackson, this is perfect."

Avery's eyes rested on the bathroom suite, and she fell instantly in love with the enormous bathtub. "This is every girl's dream—an ensuite."

Jackson ran her a bath. "The towels are over there and there is a stack of Willow's toiletries under the sink. She leaves them here for when she and Lucy visit."

Jackson left the room. Avery sat down on the king-size bed and lay back. She realised that a weight had been lifted. She felt lighter. It had been so long since she had delved deep into her past and cried so hard. Even when she told Ethan about it, the deliverance was not so heartfully told and in such detail.

CHAPTER THIRTY-EIGHT

*J*ackson got off the phone with Willow and turned when Avery entered the living room. "That was Willow checking to make sure I'm taking good care of you."

Ruby ran past her and began pulling at Jackson's trousers. "Daddy, daddy, play!"

"In a minute, sweetheart."

He turned to Avery. "I need to make a quick call to work. I won't be long. Will you watch Ruby for me?"

"Of course. Come here, Ruby."

Avery took Ruby by the hand and led them to the table where Ruby had strewn her crayons and books. Ruby grabbed a crayon and began scribbling proudly. Avery picked up a colouring book and coloured alongside Ruby. Occasionally, Ruby would glance over at Avery's colouring and smile, and then continue scribbling.

Avery lost herself in the repetitive act, finding it therapeutic. Ruby threw down her crayon and climbed up on Avery's lap without warning. She sat there watching Avery colour until she fell asleep in her arms. Avery glanced down and observed Ruby as she slept. Her heart warmed while stroking the hair off her face. The innocence of her sleeping face arrested her emotions. A single tear tumbled down her cheek.

Jackson had been standing in the doorway, watching Avery and Ruby. His smile led up to his eyes, and he placed his hand over his heart before stepping into the room. "I'm all done. Thanks for watching her."

"It was no trouble. Quite the opposite, in fact. She is lovely, Jackson."

He glanced down at Ruby. "And comfortably asleep. You must have the magic touch. She does not sleep this easy when we're alone!"

"I'm sure that's not true!"

Jackson stretched out his arms. "Here, pass her over to me. I will put her down for a while. Trust me, enjoy the peace while you can. When she wakes up, she will be full of energy and run us both ragged."

Jackson lay Ruby down on the sofa for a nap and then joined Avery in the kitchen.

"Something smells good."

"It's my way of saying thank you for letting me stay with you and Ruby. I thought I'd make lunch for us. I hope you don't mind me taking over your kitchen?"

"Are you kidding me? This is a real treat. The only time I get this treatment is when I'm visiting my sisters."

"Good. It's about ready now. I'll plate up. You go sit over there. I got this."

Jackson sat at the table overlooking the garden and observed Avery. His heart skipped a beat. She tucked a stray hair behind her ear. Jackson noted the delicate way she held herself as she moved around in the kitchen. "You sure you don't need any help?"

"I'm sure," she said while meandering over to the table.

"Avery, this looks incredible."

"It's Indian scrambled eggs. Delicious. I caramelised the onions, added garlic, ginger, and a sprinkle of garum masala. Then I threw in a pinch of nigella seeds and added the egg mixture."

Jackson took his first mouthful and his face lit up. "This is amazing."

Avery smiled. "I'm glad you like it."

Jackson noted the tiny portion Avery dished up for herself. She took a few forkfuls and then placed her cutlery down.

"You need to eat a little more than that," suggested Jackson, concerned.

"I know. My appetite is shot since..." Avery trailed off, turning to the window.

"Hey. No rush. At least you are eating, and that's the main thing. Look, I had an idea that I wanted to run by you."

"Okay. What is it?"

"Well, I've been thinking, and I thought therapy may be a way forward for you. It did wonders for me when I lost Janine. Unloading to a stranger is far easier than unloading your thoughts to friends and family. Trust me, I know from experience. A good trauma therapist offers great coping tools to get you through your worst days. I only mention it because I overheard Dr Chaudhary suggesting it to you when he handed you a bunch of leaflets at the hospital. Have you given it any thought?"

"I haven't thought beyond the fact I'm pregnant with my dead boyfriend's child. It has taken up every inch of space in my mind. Some days I get so overwhelmed I can hardly breathe. Panic consumes me."

Jackson interrupted. "Then maybe it would help you. Please consider it. I have the number of a highly respected trauma thera-pist. She comes highly recommended. At least think about it."

Avery looked into Jackson's concerned eyes. Her eyes trailed his face and rested on a small scar under his chin that was mostly covered with stubble. Her eyes journeyed back up to his eyes and Jackson's genuine smile moved her to tears.

"Hey. What's wrong?" Jackson leapt from his chair over to her and wrapped her in a hug. "I'm sorry. I just don't know how I got so lucky. You, Willow, and Lucy. "Avery paused. She buried her head in Jackson's chest and cried for the longest time. Jackson remained silent, stroking her hair until she was all cried out.

After some time, Avery pulled away from Jackson and wiped her eyes. "Maybe you're right. Therapy could help me."

Jackson squeezed her hand. "Do you want me to arrange an appointment?"

"Okay. Yes. Is it expensive?"

"Don't worry about that. I will take care of it. Now leave it with me."

"Daddy!" called Ruby from the sofa.

Jackson rose to his feet. "My princess calls!"

Avery cupped her hands around her coffee mug and sighed with relief. Her thoughts ran through her mind—positive ones for a change. *This is something I need to do. It will be good for me. I'm so lucky to have Jackson helping me through this. I don't know how I would have gotten through this last week.*

Jackson entering the room jolted her from her thoughts. Her smile reached her eyes.

"I made the call. The therapist is called Anna. She is amazing. You will be in expert hands. Your first session is Monday at 11 am. Is that too soon?"

Surprised, Avery stood up. "Monday! That was quick. Mmm, sure."

"The thing is, I have booked a block of sessions for you over the coming weeks. But it means you will need to stay here with Ruby and me. Unless you want to travel down here weekly for your sessions. It's up to you."

"I would rather stay here for a while longer if that's okay with you. I don't want to put you out."

"You will not be putting me out. I love having you here. And I know Ruby does too."

"Then I guess I'm staying."

Jackson could hardly contain his happiness. "How about we take Ruby for a long walk across the meadow? There is a river at the end of it and she loves watching the ducks."

"I would love that."

Jackson nodded. "Then I shall rustle up a picnic for us to eat later."

* * *

Avery held Ruby's hand as they strolled through the meadow at the back of Jackson's house. Ruby let go and ran, giggling along the way.

"Ruby!" Jackson hollered.

Ruby ignored him and continued running and laughing. Jackson picked up speed and ran to catch up with her, swooping her up in his arms and spinning her around. Ruby belly-laughed, and Avery watched them. Seeing the way Jackson interacted with Ruby warmed her heart. Jackson glanced over his shoulder to check on Avery who was walking slowly behind. He mouthed, "You, okay?"

Avery smiled and nodded.

Once they reached the river. Jackson laid out the picnic, and they sat around the blanket while Ruby picked daisies. "Look Daddy!"

"Wow! Can I have one?"

Ruby tottered over to him and handed him a daisy. He kissed her on the cheek and watched as Ruby made her way over to Avery and handed her one, too.

Avery became emotional as she took the flower from Ruby. "Thank you, Ruby," she said, wiping a tear from her eye.

"Looks like someone has a fan!" commented Jackson.

Ruby sat down on Avery's lap. Jackson watched Ruby with pride and then shifted his gaze to Avery. He noted her hair blowing softly and her pale skin turn rosy in the fresh air. He had a sudden urge to swoop her up and hold her tight. Shaking his thoughts, knowing that would happen, he turned his attention to Ruby.

"Can Daddy have a hug?"

Ruby held onto Avery, giggling. "Like I said: a fan!" Jackson repeated.

Jackson watched Ruby's eyes close. He glanced at Avery feeling the weight of her earlier trauma response when he approached her in the garden. He vowed to himself to do everything he could to help Avery on her healing journey.

Ruby fell asleep on Avery's lap. Avery stroked her hair while chatting with Jackson. He surprised her with his admission of his worst mental health struggles. He delved deep and shared his darkest moments. Although she knew a great deal of Jackson's struggles, she had no idea just how much he concealed from everyone.

Jackson packed away the picnic and took Ruby from Avery. Ruby didn't open her eyes and nestled her head into his shoulders. They meandered back to the house in a comfortable silence. Now and then, Jackson shot a glance at Avery and smiled, realising that his feelings for every had just taken a sudden turn. *Nope, this can never happen. Fight them. You are friends, best friends. I am the last thing she needs: a man in her life after what she's been through.*

Avery caught his attention, and he fixed his eyes on her. She interrupted his thoughts. "Jackson?"

Jackson sprung from his thoughts. "Yes."

"Everything okay?" she asked.

Embarrassed, he offered a simple nod and walked on ahead with Ruby without explanation.

Back at the house, Jackson did everything in his power not to make eye contact. More to protect himself. He realised he was still in a vulnerable position. Having Avery around the house felt so good and he convinced himself what he was feeling was misplaced feelings.

"Right then. I am going to bathe Ruby and get her ready for bed."

"I'm tired too. I think I will run a bath and have an early night."

"Sounds like a good plan. Good night, Avery."

Avery headed up the stairs and ran herself a hot bath. She lit a candle left over from Willow's last stay and submerged her body in the water. Her hands rested on her tummy. Avery noted the bump increasing and calculated she had little time left to decide. Her thoughts flashed to Ruby, curled up on her lap, and she smiled. But then swiftly turned to Ethan lying at the bottom of the staircase. *How can I do this? The baby will be a permanent reminder of what happened. I will never get away from it. What would I tell the baby once it's grown? It's unfair to them and to me. I'm not ready to be a mother. I can't do this. I just can't.*

CHAPTER THIRTY-NINE

*A*very fidgeted in her chair. She watched as the therapist organised her pen and pad on the desk. "Hello Avery. My name is Anna. I want you to know that anything you share with me in our sessions is strictly confidential."

Avery immediately warmed to Anna. She had a gentle way about her. A short, raven-coloured bob framed her oval face, accentuating her high cheekbones. Anna's smile was genuine and kind, and she defied her fifty-five years, looking more like forty-five.

Anna asked a series of questions about Avery's current mental health. "Now we have that out of the way. Start from where you feel comfortable."

Avery nodded anxiously. She glanced at Anna, who offered an encouraging smile.

"I believed I was broken for so long. That this was as good as it was going to get. Ethan made me believe so." Avery paused, reached over the desk for her glass of water and took a sip. Then continued.

"I only wanted genuine love, but I'd only known false representations of it. As a child and as an adult, I didn't know what genuine love looked like. I only knew pain and fear. So, when a veiled love presented itself to me, I embraced it with open arms. So desperate was I to be enveloped in love and kindness that the negative signs alluded me. The red flags flew beneath my radar. He caught me off guard like an enemy lurking in the shadows, ready to assail its prey."

Avery expelled a harsh breath and then continued.

"Over time, his words beat me down and cut deep into me like a knife. He wore me down. I began second-guessing myself. He denied saying things when I brought them up and convinced me I had heard things wrong. Ethan had a way of getting inside my head and completely reorganising the narrative of past arguments, convincing me he was right, and I was wrong. It was as if I was walking blind, constantly feeling around for a way forward and always heading in the wrong direction with no rhyme or reason. That is the best way I can explain it. I could always sense when he was spoiling for an argument, and I would walk away into another room. But he would follow me, calling me ignorant, attacking me emotionally, anything to get a rise out of me. Reminding me I was lucky to have him, and everyone thought so too. I believed him because I felt so little about myself. When you hear negative things about yourself constantly, you come to believe them. I am ashamed and angry for being so easily drawn into his fictitious world. Because when all said and done that is exactly what it was—fictitious, make believe, a world of his creation that I was drawn into blindly."

Anna wrote some notes. "Narcissists are highly intelligent people, Avery. They get inside their victim's head. They rewrite situations to please themselves, thus convincing the victim they were wrong. It is the very nature of who they are. They believe they can never be wrong and that it is always the other person who is at fault. They are experts in conflict. They commonly use phrases like: *that never happened, you are too sensitive, I never said that, you are wrong, it's your fault.* If you have no proof, they will have you second-guessing yourself. Gaslighting is their sword. The weaker more vulnerable someone is, the easier they will be to gaslight and manipulate. Unfortunately, Avery, you were the perfect partner in that sense for Ethan. He knew your weaknesses and weaponised them."

Avery lowered her eyes to the floor while mulling over Anna's words. "I knew nothing of narcissism. I didn't realise there was even a name for people like that. It was only afterwards, once I was free of him, that I learned Ethan was a narcissist. I was vulnerable and naïve. Ethan saw that in me and played on my weaknesses, of which there were many. He broke me down emotionally and I had no idea what was happening. I was already broken and trying so hard to leave my past behind me."

Anna made some notes. "When Jackson reached out to me, he briefed me on your past struggles, too. I think the right therapy for you is Trauma Focused Cognitive Behavioural Therapy. This form of therapy addresses PTSD in children and adults with post-traumatic stress disorder and other related trauma in relation to life events. I think you have a lot of unresolved trauma from your past that has merged with your present trauma. This is called *complex trauma*.

"How do you feel about that?"

"It sounds about right. I struggle with my past. It has overshadowed so much of my adult life. Then Ethan and what happened doubled the impact."

"Great. Now, tell me how you are feeling right now on a scale of one through to ten, one being happy and ten depressed?"

Avery mulled over Anna's question before answering. She zoned out briefly.

"Avery?"

"Sorry. Mmm, I'd say seven."

"Seven, okay. And what happened then? You seemed to drift off."

"I do that sometimes. I'm unaware I do it."

"Does it happen a lot?"

"Yes. I often zone out. Sometimes, I cut myself off from everyone. I might say I am ill, so that they will leave me alone for a day or two. Because if I say anything else, it would sound crazy."

"That is a normal trauma response. You are disassociating. It's a normal response from PTSD sufferers. We can work on that. And how are you sleeping?"

"Terrible. I have nightmares. I wake up around three or four am and I am too scared to go back to sleep."

"I can help with that. There are some mental exercises that I will talk through with you at the end of our session. I want you to put them into action each night and then let me know how you got on next week. Now, let's rewind. You were talking about the effects of your childhood. Please continue."

Avery cleared her throat. "Even now, memories of the past overwhelm me. I struggle in the darkness. The truth is, I have come to understand the darkness and the times we are forced to share. I learned to navigate these times in my own way. I never told anyone that before. Not even my closest friend, Willow."

Anna jumped in. "Sometimes, it is hard to open up your struggles to the ones closest to you. Many of my patients say they don't want to burden their loved ones. Is that a fair assumption, Avery?"

"That's exactly it. My memories of childhood often force me to retreat when thoughts of them overwhelm me. I get sad and depressed. I take a break from society until the sun shines again. I will decline invites and social engagements and at my worst, call in sick at work. That is how I have dealt with it. Up to now, it has worked for me. Willow understands that I need to be alone, and she lets me be. She doesn't pressure me at all. She just knows I am dealing with stuff."

Anna Winters studied Avery from across her desk, articulate, intelligent, and emotionally broken. Avery Masters defied her twenty-nine years and could easily pass for twenty-five. *Fragile,* she thought. She jotted down some notes, *complex trauma, trauma responses, childhood PTSD, trigger responses? Disassociates?)*

"You mentioned that your childhood was painful," she went on. "Can you expand on that for me?"

Avery fidgeted with her fingers nervously. "I was alone most of the time. Scared. I never felt like a child. I don't remember ever feeling like a child. I just recall... existing." Avery paused. Anna noticed the sadness etched over her face and the deep sorrow in her eyes.

Anna offered a comforting smile. "You're doing great, Avery. I know this is hard for you. Take your time."

Avery swiped a tear from her cheek. "Can we talk about something else?"

"Of course. Let's talk more about your life just before you met Ethan."

Avery swallowed down a lump and repositioned herself on the chair.

"Before I met Ethan, I was content with my life. I had a career I loved and bought my home. It was a struggle financially, granted, but I made it work. I did not want to rely on others for a roof over my head. That had not worked out so well for me as a child. So, after a few years of working and saving hard, I acquired a decent deposit and bought a small house. However, I did not get to enjoy my new home for long as I met Ethan soon after. It was nothing special, a basic two-bed, but it was all mine. My security. A relationship was not on my agenda. Until Ethan appeared in my life." Avery took a long pause. Again, reaching for the glass of water off the table. She glanced at the clock on the wall. "Can we continue next week?"

Anna jotted down more notes: *Memories of Ethan (trauma response–disassociates). Childhood memories (trauma response–retreats within herself)*.

"Of course. I would like to run through some mental exercises with you to aid in your sleep and nightmares before you go."

Anna talked Avery through the exercises in detail and handed her some printouts.

Anna smiled and stood up. "Same time next week?"

Avery nodded. "Yes." She reached for her bag off the floor and hunched it over her shoulder, then turned to Anna. "Thank you. See you next week."

When Avery left, Anna closed the door and sat down in her chair. Avery was marinated in pain and trauma, it weighed heavily on the therapist. She turned on her Dictaphone and recorded the session results:

"Avery Masters, age 29, session one: A great deal of underlying childhood trauma to work through, add to that her more recent PTSD born from her relationship with Ethan Channing. Avery Masters is dealing with complex post-traumatic stress disorder (C-ptsd) or acute PTSD. I was aware during the session that Avery dissociated from the conversation several times (*trauma response)* next week I would like to take her back to her childhood and work forward from there. Understanding Avery's childhood and her obvious trauma as a result of abuse is key to helping her with her current trauma. End session."

CHAPTER FORTY

*J*ackson opened the door and stood back. Avery walked through and dropped her bag on the console table.

"How'd did your appointment with Anna go?"

Avery slipped off her coat. "It went okay, I think."

Sensing she did not want to talk about it, he changed the subject. "I rustled up lunch for us. You hungry?"

Avery offered an endearing smile. "Sounds great. I will just wash my hands."

Jackson recognised Avery's distant demeanour: she was retreating again. But now he understood why. After Avery revealed the extent of her past to him, he wondered how on earth she had survived it. An overwhelming urge to protect her washed over him.

Ruby tottered up to Avery when she joined them in the kitchen. She tugged on Avery's jumper and held up her arms.

Jackson smiled. "I think someone wants to sit on your lap."

Avery picked up Ruby and sat her down on her lap. Ruby reached up to her hair and wrapped a strand around her fingers, while smiling up at her. She shot a glance at Jackson. "Well, Ruby is too cute for words."

"Yep! And she's taken with you for sure."

Instinctively, Avery placed a hand over her stomach. Jackson noticed but did not want to draw attention to it. He picked Ruby up and placed her in the highchair.

"Time for dinner young lady."

For a moment, Avery was elsewhere in her mind, still cradling her stomach. Jackson holding up a dish and calling her name forced her back to the present moment. "One scoop or two?" he asked.

"Oh, just one, please."

"One scoop it is," he said while handing her a plate.

Avery remained quiet through lunch. Ruby filled the silences chattering for the three of them. Jackson glanced at Avery from time to time, noting how quiet she was.

"By the way, Willow called. I mentioned you would be staying for a while longer. She insisted on coming down to stay for a couple of days this Friday. I thought you'd like that."

Avery's face lit up. "Really. That would be lovely."

"I knew that would make you happy. I thought the four of us could do something on Saturday. Child-friendly, of course! There is a beautiful national forest nearby. It is stunning. Ruby loves it there too. I know how much you love hiking." Jackson paused. He noticed Avery attempting to conceal her tears. "Hey, just let it out, Avery. He reached across the table and placed his hand over hers.

Avery searched Jackson's kind face. "You have been so kind to me and I just feel a little overwhelmed. I just want you to know that you mean the world to me."

Jackson rose from his chair and around to Avery. "Come here," he urged, wrapping her in his arms.

After Avery was all cried out, Jackson piped up. "So, about the forest hike, are you in?"

"I'm in. It sounds perfect."

Avery observed Jackson as he attended to Ruby.

Jackson wiped her runny nose. "I think she has a cold."

Ruby coughed as she was lifted out of the highchair. Ruby

yawned widely and rubbed her eyes. "I think I'll put her down for a nap!" Ruby placed her tiny hand on Jackson's face, and he kissed her fingers. "Come on, let's take you upstairs."

Jackson turned to Avery. "I won't be long."

Avery nodded, stood, and cleared the table. She turned on the coffee machine and then reached for her phone out of her pocket and sat by the window. While scrolling through her messages, one stood out from the rest. She gasped and her phone slipped from her fingers. Jackson entered the room and ran over to her. "What's happened?"

Avery couldn't speak. She hyperventilated and knelt on the floor trying to catch her breath.

"Avery, take slow, deep breaths with me. In-out-in-out," he directed, while rubbing the base of her back. Avery's breathing slowed. She took Jackson's arm and rose to her feet and sat back down by the window. Jackson picked her phone up off the floor and handed it to her. He remained silent and sat with her until she was ready to speak. Eventually, she turned around. Her eyes trailed over Jackson's concerned face. She opened the message on her phone and handed it to Jackson without saying a word. Jackson scrolled through the message and drew in a hefty breath.

"Avery, I don't know what to say. I have no words."

Avery bust into tears. Crying painfully like a wounded animal Jackson enveloped her tightly in his arms until she was all cried out.

"I always thought when this day came that I would be unaffected. My mother broke my heart. But now..." she trailed off.

"Hey, it's understandable you feel the pain of her passing. Love her or hate her, she was your mother and that will hurt."

"But she broke my heart. She never came looking for me. It was as if I had never existed. As a child, through all the neglect, I still loved her. Even as an adult, I have never understood why children love the people that cause them so much pain, neglect, abuse and give them up without a fight."

Jackson wiped the tears from her cheeks. "Because children

simply love their parents no matter what, unconditionally. They have only experienced how they are treated. It's all they have known. They just want their parents to love them back and constantly seek their approval, even at a very young age. What you are feeling is normal, Avery."

Avery cried into his chest, bellowing her raw pain as her tears fell. Her painful cries tugged hard at Jackson's heart. He stroked her hair until she fell silent. After some time, he looked down and saw that she had cried herself to sleep. His eyes studied her pale, tear-stained skin. His feelings for Avery overwhelmed him and he brushed her cheeks with his hand, removing a stray hair from her face.

Avery's eyes flickered open and connected with Jackson's. She raised her head and released herself from his embrace. "I'm so sorry. I can't believe I fell asleep."

Jackson leapt up when he heard Ruby calling him. "I won't be a minute."

Avery scurried to the bathroom to freshen up, feeling embarrassed. She studied her reflection for some time, noting the dark circles and tired skin. Her thoughts returned to her earlier message. *Just one phone call, one message or one letter is all it would have taken. Why mum? Why did you hate me so much? I loved you. All I wanted was your love and nothing more. Now you are gone...*

Jackson rushed down the stairs with Ruby in his arms. "Avery, open the door?"

Avery rushed to open the door. "What's wrong?"

"I don't know. She's struggling to breathe."

He dashed to his car. Avery ran after them and hopped into the backseat. "Pass her to me. I will hold her."

Jackson pealed out of the driveway and raced to the children's hospital. Avery was thankful that traffic was light, and they reached the hospital within twelve minutes. Jackson threw Avery the car keys. "Can you take care of the ticket?" he asked while swooping Ruby up in his arms and running towards A&E.

"Of course. You go!"

Jackson burst through the doors and up to reception of the children's hospital. "Please help. My daughter can't breathe."

The reception pressed a button. A doctor and nurse came rushing over. They took Ruby from Jackson and rushed her through to an emergency room. Jackson gave Ruby's details to the receptionist and waited anxiously outside of the emergency room. He paced the floor, unable to be still.

Avery caught up with him. "How is she?"

"I don't know. She is in there," he pointed.

Avery glanced at the emergency room then back to Jackson. She took his hand and laced her fingers through his and squeezed tight. "You're not alone."

When the door flung open, Jackson leapt to his feet and over to the doctor.

"Is she okay?"

"She has a fever. Please, take a seat," directed the doctor.

Jackson sat down. His eyes widened. "Please, tell me she is going to be all right?"

"Ruby has bronchiolitis, and it is mostly caused by a viral infection. This causes an inflammation of the small airways in the lungs, called bronchioles that makes it harder for the child to breathe. We have brought her fever under control. There is one more thing, during our investigation, we detected a heart murmur. These are often harmless. We will need to conduct further investigations before I can commit to a diagnosis. She is stable right now. I am going to keep her in overnight for tests. Seek the cause and then decide on the solution. We will place her in the ICU where the nurses can keep around the clock observation."

"Can I stay with her? I can't go home. I need to be here."

"Yes, of course."

An orderly appeared from the emergency room, wheeling a bed. The doctor shot a glance at Jackson. "You can follow me up to the ICU."

Avery remained seated. Jackson turned to her. "Please call Willow and Lucy for me." He reached into his pocket and threw her a set of keys. "Take my car. I will call you at home later."

Avery watched Jackson with a heavy heart until he disappeared from her sight. She hurried out of the hospital, retrieved her phone, and called Willow immediately.

"Hey, how's it going?" answered Willow.

"Willow, Ruby's ill. She's in ICU at Prince Albert Children's Hospital."

"Oh, God, no! What's happened?"

"The doctor said she has bronchiolitis. But he has detected a heart murmur. She was struggling to breathe. They're keeping her in overnight for tests. That's all I can tell you."

"I'm on my way." Willow cut off.

Avery ran to the car, climbed in, paid the ticket and headed to Jackson's house. Once home, she couldn't settle. Thoughts of Ruby and her gorgeous innocent smile arrested her. "Please God. Don't take Ruby," she said aloud. Her heart filled up with pain so deep she couldn't bear it. She headed up to Ruby's bedroom and sat down on the chair in the corner of her room. She cast her eyes over Ruby's drawings, scribblings mainly. But one drawing caught her attention. She rose to her feet and made her way across the room to take a closer look. A stick figure of a man, cat, and baby. Avery's heart swelled. She glanced around Ruby's room while clutching her stomach. *I've made my decision.*

CHAPTER FORTY-ONE

*W*illow sped into Jackson's driveway. Avery rushed to the door and opened it. She ran over to Willow, and they hugged. "I'm so glad you're here, Willow. I can't bear this. I can't imagine what Jackson is going through."

"Has he called?"

Avery shook her head. "No, not yet."

"I could not stay with Jackson." She explained. "I had to leave. It's late. Visiting time is long over. We can go to the hospital in the morning. In the meantime, we can wait for Jackson to call."

Willow brushed the tears from her cheek. "You're right, of course. A strong tea is what I need."

"Coming right up," said Avery, looping Willow's arm as they headed into the house.

Avery put the kettle on while Willow messaged Jackson. "Jackson has been through so much already. This is so unfair," blurted Willow, pacing the floor.

"I know. Here, take this tea and sit down. There's nothing we can do but wait now," advised Avery.

Willow glanced across the table at Avery. "Are you okay?"

"I'm getting there. It's a process. My Mum passed," she blurted.

Willow's eyes widened. "When?"

"I only found out today. Just before we took Ruby to the hospital. My mother's current boyfriend messaged me. She passed a couple of days ago. You'd think he would've called with something like that. Her funeral is on Monday." Avery fought back her tears and turned away from Willow.

Willow leapt from her chair over to Avery and hugged her. "I'm so sorry. All this has happened in a single day. I'm guessing you haven't even had time to process it, what with Ruby in hospital. Are you going to attend the funeral?"

Avery swallowed a lump in her throat. "Yes, I have to. I need closure. I need to say goodbye. The news hurt so much, Willow. Even though we have barely been in touch for years. Why does it hurt so much?" cried Avery.

"Because she was your mother. Would you like me to go with you?"

"Yes please. I can't go alone."

"Then that's settled."

"She never tried to reconnect. I never understood that. I always hoped she would reach out and say sorry. But she never did. That's what hurts. Now she's gone."

Willow's eyes welled up. "I don't know much about your mother, but what I am sure of is that you survived an awful childhood. And despite that, you grew up to be this wonderful human being that I love dearly. You did that all by yourself. Your childhood did not harden you. Yes, it affected you. Sadly, not all parents should be parents. You can spend your whole life trying to understand your mother's reason for the things she did and did not do, and you will never truly understand."

"I know you're right. Everything you're saying makes sense. And yet the pain I'm feeling for what could have been had things been different is crushing me right now."

Avery climbed off the chair and reached for the tissue box off the countertop. She wiped the tears from her face, looked at Willow and smiled. "Here, you need one too."

Willow took the tissue. "Thanks. I'm supposed to be comforting you!"

Willow's mobile phone pinged. Their eyes darted to the phone. Willow picked it up and looked at the message.

"It's from Jackson. Ruby's fever is under control, and she remains stable. Her breathing has returned to normal. As far as the heart murmur is concerned, he will know more in the morning. Aww, he said, look after Avery. She had some sad news today and give her a hug from me."

Willow glanced at Avery. "He really cares about you. He always has."

"I know he does. He has been amazing to me this week. I don't know how I would have coped without him, to be honest. Coming to stay here has been good for me."

"Well, it seems you have been good for each other. Have you thought anymore about what you are going to do?" Willow looked pointedly at Avery's stomach.

Avery grabbed her cup and refilled it. "Yes. I am keeping the baby."

Willow's jaw dropped. "Really?"

"Before I came to stay with Jackson, I was sure I didn't want to. But being here with Ruby and Jackson and seeing the love they have for one another changed my thinking. This baby I'm carrying has done nothing wrong. And there was a time I loved Ethan despite how things turned out."

"I am so happy you decided to keep it. Know we will all be there for you."

"I know you will. I just want to be the mother to my baby that my mother wasn't to me. There is a lot of stuff for me to work through. Therapy will help with that. It's time I faced my demons and moved forward."

"Well, I'm here for it all. You will face nothing alone. Aunt Willow is at the ready." Willow stepped close and pulled Avery in a tight embrace. "I love you, Avery. Soul sisters forever."

CHAPTER FORTY-TWO

*J*ackson leapt to his feet when Dr Cavendish entered the room. "Good morning."

"Morning," Jackson answered.

Dr Cavendish pulled up a chair and brushed a mop of red curly hair off his face. "I have good news. Ruby has an innocent heart murmur. It's common in children and nothing to worry about."

Jackson's eyes widened.

Dr Cavendish continued. "It's not serious at all. What this means for Ruby is that she will not require treatment."

"So, Ruby will be okay?"

"Yes. No cause for concern and no further treatment required. Her heart murmur will not cause any issues. Here is some information on innocent murmurs for you to take away with you." He handed Jackson a handful of pamphlets. "Ruby's fever is under control, and she can go home now. Keep an eye on her temperature over the next couple of days."

"I will," Jackson agreed.

Dr Cavendish offered Jackson a reassuring smile. "Okay then, I will sign the discharge papers and you can take Ruby home."

"Thank you," said Jackson.

* * *

Jackson walked through the door with Ruby, just after ten am—much to Willow's surprise.

"What the hell?" blurted Willow.

"They discharged Ruby this morning. She has what is called an innocent heart murmur. But she can carry on as normal and no treatment required. I will explain everything to you later. I want to put Ruby to bed." Jackson's eyes darted around the room. "Where's Avery?"

"She hasn't woken up yet. We went to bed late after a long talk."

"Okay. I will be back down in a few minutes."

Jackson closed Ruby's door and walked straight into Avery on the landing. Half asleep and rubbing her eyes, she stared at Jackson as if he were a ghost. "Jackson?"

"Morning," he whispered, putting his finger to his lips, and pointing to Ruby's room.

"I will explain downstairs, but she is fine."

"Thank God. I was so worried." Avery whispered back. "I will see you downstairs in a few minutes."

Jackson caught up with Willow in the kitchen. "A strong coffee for me, Sis."

"One strong coffee coming up. Thank God Ruby is okay."

Jackson nodded. "I watched Ruby's chest rise and fall all night, in fear she may stop breathing again. It was the most painful night of my life. For a moment yesterday, I thought I might lose her, Willow. I never want to go through that again. I couldn't bear it. She is the light of my life. I love her so much it hurts."

"I know you do. That's why you are such an amazing father. At least it's not congenital like what Aunt Jenny had. Things would have been very different then. Ruby is a tough cookie, just like her dad."

"Yep. Every moment of life should be cherished. It's so fragile."

"Agreed. By the way, Avery told me about her mother. She is taking it better than I thought. She's emotional yes, but anyone would be. However, she's going to be okay."

"Avery had just received the news when Ruby took a turn yesterday. There was no time for her to process anything. Are you sure she's okay?"

"Yes, I'm sure. She also told me she's keeping the baby, too. Being here with you and Ruby helped massively in that decision."

"Wow! Well, she won't be going through it alone. She has all of us to help her. And Ruby gets a new playmate."

"I think Avery is re-evaluating herself and her life."

Avery ambled into the kitchen, poured herself a coffee and joined Willow and Jackson at the table. "So Ruby is going to be fine?"

"Yes. Thank God. It's called an innocent heart murmur. Although it felt anything but innocent yesterday. It was the viral infection that caused her breathing issue. I need to keep an eye on her temperature over the next couple of days."

"Thank God. I was beside myself with worry. I'm so thankful she is okay. You must be so relieved Jackson."

Jackson drew in a deep breath. "You have no idea how much."

Willow rose to her feet. "I have a couple of calls to make. First, to Lucy and then Mum and Dad. They are anxious for news. Back soon."

Jackson turned his attention to Avery. "You, okay?"

"I'm okay." Her eyes lowered to her stomach, and she rested her hand on it. "I have to be now that I'm going to be a mother," she smiled.

Jackson leapt from his chair over to Avery and enveloped her in a tight hug. "I'm so pleased. I am here for you. Every step of the way. I promise you."

The warmth of Jackson's arms around her made her feel safe.

Willow burst into the room and stopped in her tracks. Avery pulled away from Jackson and stood back.

Jackson spoke up. "I just heard the news about the baby."

Willow jumped in. "This is amazing. A new addition to our family is what we all need. I can't wait to tell Lucy."

Jackson cast a discreet glance at Avery. Her face glowed, and she had never looked more beautiful to him than at this moment. Willow glanced over and caught the moment, smiling to herself. She looked over at Avery and back at Jackson. Jackson realised Willow knew and a knowing smile exchanged between them.

"I'm going to rustle up lunch for us. Why don't you two take a walk in the meadow? I think you both need some fresh air after the last twenty-four hours. I will listen out for Ruby. Lunch will be an hour," suggested Willow.

Jackson turned to Avery. "What do you think?"

"Mmm, yes, sure. I could do with some fresh air."

Willow smiled inwardly and began prepping lunch. Avery and Jackson pulled on their trainers, grabbed their coats, and left.

As they approached the meadow, Avery gasped. "This is such a beautiful place. If I lived here, I would spend all my time in this meadow taking photos."

"You are welcome to come visit anytime. Consider it your second home," Jackson offered.

Avery laughed. "I don't even have a first home right now. I have so much to consider now. I need a home for the baby."

"My advice is don't get hung up on the small stuff. Everything will fall into place. Take one day at a time. And you have two homes: Willow's, and mine. We are in this together. I mean that."

Avery surprised Jackson. She inched closer to him and planted a warm kiss on his cheek. "Thank you for everything. You're like my own personal angel."

Jackson blushed. And without thinking, he weaved his fingers through Avery's as they walked. It took a moment before he realised it. Avery looked down at their entwined hands. Jackson released his fingers and pulled away.

"I'm so sorry. It was automatic. I don't know what I was thinking."

Avery didn't say a word about it. Instead, she switched the subject. "I have decided to go to my mother's funeral. Willow is coming with me. I didn't want to attend alone. Would you like to come, too?"

Confused about what had just happened, Jackson searched Avery's face intently. Avery turned away and looked ahead. He realised Avery did not want to talk about it and respected that. "Yes, I would. When is it?"

"Monday. I have the address on my phone. It's about one hour, thirty minutes from here."

"That's not too far. How do you feel about it?"

"I am reconciled with it. Initially, it was a shock. I just want closure and saying goodbye will give me that." Avery placed her hand over her tummy. "I need to move forward and be strong for this one."

CHAPTER FORTY-THREE

*M*onday arrived fast. Avery was the last to leave the graveside. Only a handful of people attended the funeral. Avery stood at the back with Willow and Jackson. A deep sadness cloaked her. She waited for the mourners to leave and stepped up to the graveside and looked down at the lowered coffin. She knelt and cried for the longest time.

Jackson stepped forward, but Willow held him back. "Leave her be. She needs to do this part alone. She needs to say goodbye. I know it's painful to watch and see her like this."

Jackson turned away from Willow and hugged Ruby. Willow tapped his arm. "Hey, I know you're in love with Avery. It's clear as day."

Jackson nodded and swiped a tear from his face. "I am. Is it that obvious?"

"To me, yes. But it's not the right time, Jackson. Avery has so much to work through emotionally."

"I know this. Don't think for one minute I haven't thought all this through. I know it is not our time. But the day will come when it will be. I am a patient man. I love her, Willow, and I want to be there for her no matter what. Right now, she needs a friend, and I am here for that."

"No one would be happier to see the two people I love most in the world come together."

Avery looked down into the shallow grave, weeping. "Mum, I forgive you. I am going to be a mother too. My baby will only know love. I'm sad you could not give me that. I hope you have peace now. Goodbye, Mum."

Avery through a handful of dirt onto the coffin and made to stand.

Willow noticed Avery rising from her feet. "Come on, I think she's ready to go."

Avery walked over to Willow and Jackson. "I'm good to go. I'm going to be fine."

Avery started walking ahead. Jackson shot a glance at Willow as they both turned and looked at Avery confused and surprised.

Jackson whispered. "Do you think she's okay? She seems calm and collected for the first time?"

"I think she has found closure. Coming here today was symbolic for her. She got to put her past to rest and say goodbye. I'm guessing she has some clarity for the first time in her life. Avery is going to be just fine. Come on, let's catch her up."

CHAPTER FORTY-FOUR

(Six months later)

*A*very smiled from ear to ear. Tears of happiness streamed her face. Jackson observed her cradling her baby. "Hey, I'm your mummy. You are going to be cherished always. I promise you."

Avery turned to Jackson. "Come closer."

Surprised, Jackson inched his chair closer. Avery held out her baby for Jackson.

"Are you sure?" he asked.

"Of course. I want you to."

Jackson took the tiny baby in his arms and looked at her minute fingers and held onto one. His eyes darted up at Avery. "She's beautiful. Just like her mama."

Avery reached out her hand and wrapped it around Jackson's. "Thank you for guiding me through these last six months. I couldn't have done it without you."

Jackson's eyes darted from the baby in his arms and back to Avery. He held her gaze and teared up. Avery squeezed his hand tight once more. "I know, Jackson."

Confusion crossed Jackson's face. "Know what?"

Avery leaned forward and kissed him softly on the lips. "I know!"

Their fingers laced in and out together. A knowing silence between them spoke loud and clear. Avery searched his eyes. "We need to come up with a name. Together." Her eyes darted to her baby.

"Really?"

"Yes, together. I love you too, Jackson."

Jackson handed the baby to Avery, moved onto the bed and enveloped her in his arms. "You have made me the happiest man alive. I promise you this, you will never know pain with me, only love. I will cherish you both always. I love you."

He leaned in and placed his warm plump lips on hers. Then Willow burst into the room!

"Well, finally! This is the best day ever. You two are my favourite people."

Jackson climbed off the bed and hugged Willow. "Thanks, Sis."

Willow whispered in his ear. "I'm happy for you."

"I will give you some girl time. Do you need anything from the canteen?"

Avery and Willow shook their heads and Jackson headed out of the room.

"So, Jackson, hey!"

"Are you okay with it? What with Jackson being your brother and all?"

"Are you kidding me? I think it's great. I always thought you would end up together. Jackson has liked you for the longest time. You are right for one another. Look, Avery, no one will treat you as well as Jackson will. He is literally the perfect guy. Of course, I'm biased, him being my brother and all!"

Avery reached for Willow's hand. "Now I know what genuine reciprocal love feels like."

* * *

While walking along the corridor, Jackson noticed a sign on the wall: *Chapel.* He paused at the door for a while. An old man exited through the door and looked at Jackson. "He won't bite. Go in."

Jackson entered the chapel. It was empty except for one lit candle at the front. Jackson walked to the front, knelt, and clasped his hands together.

"I'm not one for praying much. Can't recall the last time I went to church. I felt compelled to walk through this door today. My feet kind of carried me forward. I simply wanted to say thank you."

Jackson stayed for a brief time, lit a candle, and left sporting a huge smile.

ALSO BY D.G. TORRENS

AMNESIA
(Romantic Suspense)

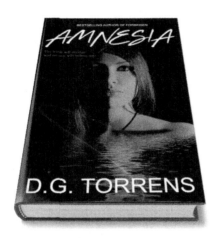

FINDING YOU
(Romantic Suspense)

<u>Biographies & Memoirs</u>
Amelia's Story (A childhood Lost book 1.)
Amelia's Destiny (Finding my way Book 2.)
Amelia The Mother (A pocket full of innocence Book 3.)

<u>Romantic/Suspense</u>
Amnesia (Romantic suspense
Finding You (Romantic suspense)
Tears of Endurance (Ferria/fielding novel 1.)
Whispers from Heaven (Ferria/fielding novel 2.)
Forbidden (Hamilton/Sharma novel 1.)
Dissolution (Hamilton/Sharma novel 2.)
Unforeseen) Hamilton/Sharma novel 3.)

<u>Military Romance</u>
Broken Wings
A Soldier's Fear
The Poppy Fields (Book 1.)
The Poppy Fields-*Eternity bound* (Book 2.)
The Poppy Fields- *In life we trust* (Book 3.

<u>Poetry & Prose</u>
Abyss (Journey through depression)
Sonder (Thought provoking poetry & prose)
Military Boots (Anthology of war poetry)
Heart and Mind

<u>Quotes</u>
Midnight Musings (300 life quotes)

ABOUT THE AUTHOR

D.G. Torrens–is a UK/USA international bestselling Author/Poet/screenwriter from Birmingham UK. D.G. has written and published more than 20 multi-genre books over the last decade.

D.G. is represented by Hershman Rights Management (HRM Literary Agents).

A prolific writer with a deep passion for the written word, D.G. is a founding member of AuthorcityUK and Bestsellingreads.com. The author recently took part in a 4-part TV interview with AuthorPaedia TV Live in the USA. You can catch the episodes on YouTube.

D.G's books can be found on all Amazon sites worldwide.

If you enjoyed ONE FOR SORROW, try AMNESIA or FINDING YOU (psychological romantic thrillers)

The author loves to connect with her readers. To connect with the author, you can visit her at the following links:

Twitter: www.twitter.com/torrenstp
Website: www.dawnsdaily.com
Amazon USA: www.amazon.com/dgtorrens
Amazon UK: www.amazon.co.uk/dgtorrens
Bookbub: D.G. Torrens Books - BookBub
Bestsellingreads.com: D.G. Torrens - BestSelling Reads

Printed in Great Britain
by Amazon

21930887R00131